ALVINA

Strong and Determined

Based on a true story

Kay Marie Perrin

Dedicated to

My grandmother, Alvina Frieda William Hursting

and

My mother, Naoma Bertha Hursting

Table of Contents

Chapter 1

By late summer, the whispers weren't whispers anymore. They carried through open windows, hung in the still air over backyard fences, and rode the creaking floorboards of porches like dust in a draft.

The gossip about Mary Selm and George Williams had spread, settled, and grown thick like mildew.

"Her husband's not even dead yet," said the shortest woman of the group.

"I heard that Oscar died yesterday."

"Who told you?"

"I heard the same news at the pharmacy."

"Well, even if he died, Mary is sinning."

"Oscar's not even in the ground," the oldest of the bunch muttered.

It was Saturday. Four women, all older, all seasoned in the art of porch judgment, sat beneath the faded awning like queens without courts. The fifth presence, a small boy, went unnoticed, crouched quietly at the edge of the steps, his legs swinging and ears wide open.

"Look at him go," the short woman continued. "Every Saturday like this. Same hammer. Same ladder. Different excuse."

A steady clank of metal on wood echoed from across the road. George Williams, with rolled sleeves, was hard at work again, though no one quite knew what was more.

"What's he doing this time?" asked the plumpest of the women.

"I'll tell you what he's doing. He's digging that tunnel."

"Digging what?"

One of the women pointed across the street, towards a slim structure that connected two houses like a wooden spine. It was a low, boxy passageway, barely tall enough for a grown man to walk within, which wove through the near side yard that had previously separated the Selm house from the Williams house.

"They're calling it a 'hallway,'" the short woman said, eyes narrowing. "But everyone knows it's a tunnel. A tunnel built for shame."

"Who connects two houses like that? They're not kin. Not properly."

"Oscar's not even in the ground," the oldest of the bunch muttered, again like a scratched record.

"Mary's got nerve, I'll say that." The short woman reached for her cane, using it to point towards one of the houses. "Look at the paint. Same color, same trim, same shingles on the roof. She's matching the houses now. Trying to pass them off as one."

"They've erased the line. The whole street used to know where her place ended and his began."

Not anymore. Now there was only this strange, liminal passage connecting them. A symbol of something everyone saw but no one wanted to name.

"She says it's for the children, so that they don't have to run through the yard in winter. Says it'll keep them warm."

"Warm?" the heavy-set woman scoffed. "You know what else it keeps warm."

Laughter, sharp and knowing, burst from the porch.

The young boy alone didn't laugh. Sitting on the porch steps, he watched the man work his steady hands, the rhythm of his hammer, the way he knelt and leaned and measured twice before doing about anything. He didn't understand what shame had to do with roofs or hallways – he only knew that something big was being built—something he'd never seen before.

"I heard the judge refused to perform the ceremony. Said it wasn't proper. They were mired in circumstance, so they planned to go to the county clerk and get him to sign it. No church, no flowers, no witnesses but the clerk."

"That's what this marriage is now, some paperwork."

"They used to be invited places," the tall woman said. "Now people change the subject when Mary walks into a room."

"The ladies auxiliary didn't even ask her to bake for the church bazaar. Imagine that. Mary Selm, left off the pie list."

"She chose George over the pie list."

"They're not joined at the hip now, either," the short woman added. "They're sealed at the foundation."

A pause fell over the porch, thick and self-satisfied.

"Her children still go to school with mine," the tall woman finally said. "But none of the other mothers invite them over anymore. It's not the children's fault. Still, people don't forget."

"No, they don't."

George moved down the far side of the tunnel roof, measuring out another plank. The boy leaned forward on the steps, watching intently.

Clink. Six seconds. Clink. Six more. Clink.

The boy blinked slowly, the rhythm steady in his chest now. He didn't know what kind of love needed a tunnel, but it sounded like something that lasted longer than a pie list.

By the end of the week, people had stopped waving to George. Shopkeepers looked past Mary as though she weren't there, and at church, her pew sat conspicuously empty. Children began whispering behind their hands whenever either of them passed by in the street. One neighbor stopped sending her boys to play with the Selm children. Many soon followed.

By the time Mary and George got married - quietly without a pastor, without flowers, without family- only one neighbor had offered a dish for their potluck reception. Most of the town pretended the event never happened.

"Shameless," said the short woman, clutching her prayer book the following Sunday. "Just shameless."

In the months following the marriage, Mary began to recede from the public eye. Her sole responsibility became keeping up the two houses, and with the tunnel built, she didn't need to take a step outside to do this. When George's sons began to fetch the groceries for her, people assumed she had taken the proper step of putting herself into a self-enforced exile for her sins. By the time a year had passed, people slowly began to move on to other rumors, the Williams-Selms family providing them with too little new material to work with. Those who talked of Mary did more speculating than judging, debating one another as to what had happened to the woman. The most popular theory was that she'd secretly become an invalid, struck down by some holy act of retribution days after the wedding. Still more forgot about Mary entirely, imagining the empty pew she'd left behind had always sat absent on Sunday mornings.

That was, until a portly-looking woman made her way into that pew nearly eighteen months after the wedding. Her face altered by the change in her body, her skin pale from having gone out so little for so long, many of the churchgoers didn't recognize her at first. They might not have noticed her at all, had her oldest daughter not sat with her before the sermon started. But soon the dots began to connect, and by the time the sermon ended, Williams' fate was sealed.

"There's no doubt," said one of the town's few midwives, eying the woman's belly.

A couple of the younger ladies nearly ran out of the church as the pastor finished the sermon, dying to tell someone, anyone, of the unthinkable transgression they'd seen.

Chapter 2

Though she'd gone to the church to speak of baptismal matters with the pastor, the town soon raged over how Mary had not repented for her sins but had gone as far as pridefully showing off its fruits in the house of God.

Many wrote the baby off as doomed before it left the womb. When the name Alvina Frieda Williams appeared in the church bulletin two weeks later, printed at the bottom, misspelled, beneath a request for hymnals and a notice about the chicken supper, people talked of how ugly the name was. They could only imagine what the baby might become. In the next twenty years, not a single girl in the town would be named Alvina.

"I suppose she'll raise the girl in that tunnel house like nothing's wrong," the tall woman said on the porch. The others nodded or said nothing at all.

And so, Alvina learned to crawl in a house where the footsteps were quiet, and the curtains stayed drawn. She took her first steps somewhere in the middle of the hallway between the homes, balanced between two worlds the town refused to recognize as one.

Mary sewed her dresses by hand. George built her a wooden cradle, carved with her initials at the head. Her siblings step, half, and otherwise loved her fiercely. The family became more whole because of her, a unifying object that branched into the worlds of all through their common relation to the one.

But outside their walls, the world did not soften. At Alvina's baptism, only family members filled the pews. Though George had invited nearly every one of his old work friends, most had other engagements, and every 'maybe' or 'we'll see' had rung as an empathic 'no' in that nearly empty church. Even the pastor didn't linger after the final hymn.

Alvina remembered those early years with an odd clarity. Not warmth, exactly, but steadiness. She remembered the tunnel smelling of cedar and lemon oil. She remembered how the smell of wood clung to George every time he came back after work, how her mother's hands were always busy with chores. She remembered how her siblings would raise her high in the air and carry her through both houses until her ribs hurt from laughter.

She also remembered that people walked faster past her and her mother whenever they passed them on the sidewalk. She remembered how older kids looked at her sideways in church, and younger ones pointed at her when they thought she wasn't looking.

Outside of the house, there was one person who always talked to George, Mary, and Alvina if he saw them on the street or in a store - the boy from the porch all those years ago. He always tipped his hat to Mary and bent down to greet little Alvina as if she were royalty.

"Well now," he'd say with a warm smile, "aren't you growing like a sapling in spring?"

Alvina would beam and hide behind her mother's skirt, peeking out enough to give him a little wave. The boy, much older now, would talk to Mary as best as he could, if only to catch more glimpses of the little girl here and there. If the rest of the town saw Alvina's unique circumstances of her upbringing as the surefire cause of her doom, the boy felt that these circumstances were instead proof that the little girl was destined for bigger things. One day, Mary went as far as asking the boy's grandmother, one of the ladies on the porch, if her grandson might like to come over and play with Alvina sometime, who saw so few kids anywhere close to her age. The lady gave an answer, then straightforwardly told Mary she'd have to leave because "I'd prefer if others didn't see us talking like this."

The next day, a note in a neat woman's handwriting was left at Williams' door. It said that the boy's family had gone abroad last week, that the grandmother didn't know when the family would be coming back, and that it would be appreciated if Williams did not talk to her again about the matter. Neither Mary nor Alvina ever saw the boy after that.

By the time she was six, Alvina had learned more than her letters and numbers. During her first year of school, she had learned how to read rooms, how to sense when adults grew quiet after her name was mentioned, and how to walk through spaces that seemed colder the moment she entered. Still, her world at home was rich in its quiet way.

She remembered George's heavy boots, always thudding across the floor before dawn. He was always kind to her, but they did not share the closeness she would continue to develop with her mother. Though he was as much her father as Mary was her mother, George rarely spoke to Alvina with anything more than nods, and never quite figured out how to cradle her the way he once had his older children. He built things for her, a bookshelf, a little chair with her name carved into the back but could not comfort her when she cried or asked questions about the world outside their house. Though he would've refused to admit it, public opinion had shaken George's confidence in his paternal abilities, and he often felt staying away from Alvina was the best thing he could do for her.

"I think Dad forgets I'm here," she whispered once to Mary, after George passed her without a glance.

Mary cupped her daughter's chin gently, drawing her into her lap. "No, sweetheart. He sees you. He doesn't know how to show it."

Then she rocked Alvina gently back and forth, as she had since infancy.

"We both see you every day."

But George's self-imposed distancing pushed Alvina further into Mary's arms with each passing year, and soon the child's mother became her only compass in a world without maps. She brushed Alvina's thick hair each morning before school, tied it back with ribbons she stitched herself, and packed her lunches with notes tucked into folds of wax paper.

Later in life, when Alvina would look back on the past to better understand her present, a single memory of early childhood always found its way to the surface. In her first year at school, she had overheard a female classmate whispering cruel things behind cupped hands as Alvina returned from the bathroom. Even when she was well into middle age, Alvina could remember the fury with which she flung her little book satchel onto the floor after returning from school that afternoon.

Mary soon discovered she was lying face-down in bed, her pillow damp with tears.

"They said we live in a tunnel like rats," Alvina cried when her mother asked her what was wrong. Saying it aloud had made her tremble even more, from shame more than anger. Alvina didn't realize how much she was convulsing until Mary sat down beside her on the bed and put her head in her mother's lap.

She caressed her daughter's cheek for a few minutes, letting her calm down a bit.

"Let them think what they want," Mary finally ventured to say once Alvina had all but stopped shaking. "But you listen to me, this house may have a tunnel, but we don't crawl. We walk proudly. We walk knowing who we are."

"But why do they say those things? And why don't they treat me the same as everyone else or play with me?"

"Because they're afraid," Mary said. "And when people are afraid, they build fences out of silence and pretend they're safe inside. But you and I, we build bridges even if they never walk across them."

Later that night, Mary tucked Alvina into bed and pulled out the old storybook with the broken spine. It was one of the few books the family possessed, and the only one Alvina ever read. That night, as many other nights, Mary read Alvina's favorite story aloud to her, one about a girl who lives in the woods and builds her house out of fallen branches.

When Mary finished, she laid the book down and whispered, "Alvina, you're like her, you know. Strong, determined, clever, and brave."

"Even if I don't have friends?"

Mary brushed a strand of hair from her daughter's face.

"Friends will come. But for now, you have me."

Alvina fell asleep with her mother's hand still wrapped around hers.

Chapter 3

At fifteen, Alvina had started keeping quiet about things that used to bubble out of her without thought, but not about her mother. Not now.

When she was six, she was still all questions and chatter. Mary had been the center of her small world, then the one who answered every curiosity with patience and a soft smile. If Alvina asked why the moon followed her home, Mary would point to the sky and explain gravity in the simplest words she could. If Alvina wondered why some children didn't wave back on the playground, Mary would say, "Sometimes people forget how to be kind. But we don't."

Each morning before school, Mary warmed Alvina's socks on the stove and knelt to slip them over her small feet. "Your toes are icicles," she'd tease, humming the lullaby she'd sung since Alvina was a baby. "If I put these on any slower, you'll be late for school, and I'll be jailed for negligence."

Alvina would giggle, cradling her schoolbooks. "Then I'll visit you every day and bring my spelling words. You can quiz me through the bars."

Their bond had been stitched together by small, steady things, shelling peas in the backyard, plucking wild mint for tea, collecting buttons from old shirts to string into bracelets. Mary taught her to hem handkerchiefs, to slice apples without cutting her fingers, to light a match and strike it fast enough to make a flame. On Saturdays, when they had a few coins, they'd walk to the corner store hand in hand. Mary always wore her frayed straw hat, and Alvina, even at ten, still reached for her mother's hand when they crossed the street, though she glanced around first to see if anyone was looking.

She didn't have many close friends. Not really. There were girls at school who passed notes and laughed at recess, but no one shared secrets with her. Mary was her person, the one she whispered to in the kitchen after dinner while drying the dishes, the one who knew which dreams still haunted her and how she liked her breakfast eggs. It wasn't that Alvina didn't want friends; it was that none of the girls understood her, and she didn't quite understand them.

Her stepsiblings were all older. The closest in age was five years ahead and was always buried in his radio parts or helping George in the workshop. The others had jobs or lives that pulled them away. Even when they were home, they didn't talk to her much. When they did, it was in a careful tone, as if they weren't sure what kind of sister she was supposed to be. The truth was, she didn't feel like a sister to them. She felt like a shadow tucked behind Mary's apron.

George, her stepfather, was kind but distant. He never raised his voice, but he never sat beside her to ask about her day. He'd ruffle her hair in passing or hand her a slice of toast without comment. Once, when she was eight, she got a splinter in her palm and tried to hide the tears. George noticed and wordlessly pulled her hand toward him, used his pocketknife to work it out gently, and then wrapped her palm in a clean strip of gauze. He never said a word, and neither did she, but she remembered the way he patted her head afterward. Their relationship was quiet, practical, dependable, but never warm in the way she shared with Mary.

At school, things changed as she grew older. When she was seven, a boy tripped her in the hallway and called her "the whisper-baby," a name she never understood but that stuck for weeks. When she was nine, a pair of girls cornered her in the bathroom and asked if it was true that her mother had married the blacksmith while her husband was still alive. She didn't know how to answer. She stood there, flushed and silent, until they laughed and walked away. From then on, she avoided the bathroom during recess.

She had no close friends to confide in, not really. Not ever.

There were classmates, yes. Faces she saw every day, girls who knew her name, boys who sometimes muttered it with a smirk or an eyeroll. But no one spoke to her with kindness or sat beside her at lunch by choice. No one asked if she was all right on the days she came to school with red eyes.

By ten, she had stopped trying to sit near the other girls during recess. They never said she couldn't, but they never made room. When she lingered too close, the conversation would shift, smiles would tighten, eyes would glance elsewhere. When she walked away, laughter followed.

By eleven, she had grown quiet. She stopped raising her hand in class unless she was sure she was right. She kept her eyes low when other girls whispered and giggled. If she overheard her name, she pretended she didn't. Her books became her best company. She carried paperbacks in her coat pocket and read between classes, on the porch swing, and in the stairwell before the first bell rang.

For Alvina, age twelve brought a growth spurt and new awkwardness. Her limbs felt too long for her clothes, and she began worrying that her voice sounded too high or too flat. She started ironing her blouse before school, like Mary had taught her, and checked her reflection twice before leaving the house. Still, classmates teased her about her old shoes, her homemade lunches, and the way she didn't go to the school dances.

Also, at twelve her desk was in the back corner of the classroom. The teacher assigned seats alphabetically, but even that felt intentional, like the universe knew she needed to be out of sight. Her hand rarely went up anymore. When it did, the teacher seemed surprised, and the other students barely looked up. When she got the answer right, no one nodded or whispered, "Good job." When she got it wrong, someone always snorted.

Thirteen brought a bitter awareness. She noticed how boys looked past her. She saw how girls paired off and pulled away. Once, a boy in her homeroom started calling her "the undertaker's daughter," a name that made no sense but stuck anyway. He said it was because she looked like she was always attending a funeral. The others laughed. Alvina didn't flinch. Not anymore.

She ate her lunch alone. Always alone. The far end of the bench is near the window, where the breeze sometimes carried in the sound of traffic or distant birds. It was a reminder that there was a world beyond school. Her lunches were plain now. A cold potato sandwich or bread with lard, packed quickly each morning with whatever she could scavenge. Mary had packed them until that year, always cutting the crusts off, always slipping in a folded napkin and a scribbled note: *Think strong, my girl. You are.*

Fourteen was quieter. She stopped asking to invite anyone over and no longer talked about what she was reading. But every evening, Mary still waited in the kitchen, apron dusted with flour, asking gently, "How was school, sweetheart?"

But because Mary had fallen ill, there were no more notes. No more warm bread wrapped in a dishcloth. No more crustless edges. Just cold food and colder silences.

The usual chatter around her about older boys, about dances, about the new girls in town floated past like voices in a language she no longer understood. No one asked her opinion. No one asked her anything.

Once, in eighth grade, a teacher pulled her aside after class and said, "You know, you could try smiling more. It might make the other girls feel more comfortable around you."

Alvina had nodded without meeting her eyes. She hadn't smiled much since.

Home was different until it wasn't. Mary was the only one who truly *saw* her. Not just in passing, but fully. She asked questions no one else bothered with: "What did the sky look like when you walked to school?" "What made you feel small today?" "What made you feel big?"

Even when Alvina only answered with shrugs, Mary would hum and nod as if she'd spoken volumes.

With her stepsiblings, there was no such connection. They were older and lived in a different orbit. Theo spent his evenings with soldering irons and transistor parts, and the others treated her like an inconvenience. Not unkind, just…uninterested. As if she were a neighbor's child left behind too long.

George was steady but silent. He provided and nodded when she passed but rarely said more than a few words to her. She didn't blame him. She wasn't quite his daughter, not the way the older brothers were.

She knew that if Mary were gone, there would be no one left who knew her at all. Truly.

So, she bore the teasing, the isolation, the sideways glances, and sudden silences when she entered a room. She grew used to the idea that people would forget her name before they ever remembered to learn it.

Shortly after Alvina turned fifteen, she began noticing changes in her mother. Mary's walk, which had always been quick and decisive, started to slow down. Her voice also changed, initially gradually, then quickly, until she grew as raspy as wind through dry reeds within a month. But in the end, it was the persistent cough that rattled in Mary's chest from dawn until dusk that pushed Alvina to act.

"Did you sleep, Mama?" Alvina asked her mother one morning as the two sat down for breakfast.

Mary managed to smile.

"Like a log."

"But you were coughing all night. I could hear you from my room."

Mary shrugged, brushing at her shawl.

"It's a tickle in my chest, that's all. Nothing to worry about, sweetheart."

Alvina knitted her brows subconsciously.

"Ma, I want you to go see Dr. Brill."

Mary shook her head.

"Alvina, I know you're worried, but we can't afford to go see Dr. Brill every time I have a cold."

"It's not a cold," Alvina said in the firmest tone she could manage. "You know you're getting sicker every day."

Mary's answer was to begin eating again, and soon they were both in silence once more. But the words lingered in the minds of both long after they left the table.

The next afternoon, before Alvina got home from school and George was at the blacksmith shop, there was a knock at the door.

Mary was sitting at the kitchen table in her robe, a teacup untouched before her, when she heard it, her heart sank.

Not now. Not today. Not after she'd told Alvina no.

The knock came again, this time sharper.

She rose too quickly, clutching the table for balance. Her breath caught in her chest.

"I told her not to," she muttered, dragging her feet toward the door. "Lord help me, I said to that child not to."

When she opened it, Alvina and Dr. Brill stood there.

The old physician gave Mary a solemn nod and stepped inside without waiting for an invitation. He carried his black bag in one hand; his hat tucked under the other arm. Alvina looked pale but resolute, her lips pressed into a flat, guilty line.

"I'm sorry, Mama," she said quietly.

Mary's eyes, darkened by fever, settled on her daughter. "You went behind my back."

"I know," Alvina said, voice breaking. "But I had to."

Dr. Brill was already unpacking his stethoscope. "Let's not waste time with apologies. Sit down, Mary."

Mary's protest died in her throat. She didn't have the strength to argue.

She let herself be guided to the nearest chair. Alvina hovered behind her, watching every breath her mother took as if counting them.

Dr. Brill listened to her chest for a long time, moving the stethoscope in careful increments. He tapped her ribs. He asked how long she'd had the cough, how long the fevers had been coming at night, and how she'd been sleeping.

Finally, he leaned back and exhaled through his nose, his mouth tightening. Then he looked Mary in the eye.

"Mary, you need to be admitted to the hospital. Today," he said. His voice was gentle, but there was no softening in the words. "You've got pneumonia. We've ruled out tuberculosis, but pneumonia in your condition…" He hesitated. "There's no treatment I can offer you at home."

Mary closed her eyes briefly. "How long?"

He didn't answer right away. His silence was answering enough.

"I see," she said quietly.

Alvina sank onto the chair across from her mother, her voice thick with fear. "Why didn't you tell me it was this bad?"

"I didn't want you worrying," Mary murmured. "You have school and chores. If I told you… It would've swallowed you whole."

"I don't care about school," Alvina said. "You're all I have."

Mary reached across the table, her hand trembling as she took Alvina's. "You're braver than I ever was," she said. "You did the right thing."

Alvina looked down at their hands, one warm and dry, the other cold and trembling. She could still see the faint white scars on Mary's knuckles from years of laundry and scrubbing, and cooking for too many mouths with too little rest.

"You should've told me," she whispered.

"I didn't want you to feel alone," Mary said. "And now you won't. You have George. You have your older siblings."

"No," Alvina said. "I have you."

Dr. Brill stood, his face softening. "I'll take you to the hospital in my buggy outside. You'll need to pack a few things. I have plenty of blankets."

Mary nodded and pushed her teacup away. The strength in her was slipping, but her eyes were clear. "Alvina, please pack a small bag for me. I don't plan on staying long."

Neither of them said what they both knew.

The hospital was six blocks from their house, but in winter it felt like miles. The next afternoon, Alvina made the walk in her thin, well-worn coat, the wind biting through the fabric and turning her cheeks raw. The paper mask the nurse gave her fogged her breath and chafed her skin, but she never complained. She came as often as she could, even if only to sit beside her mother for a few quiet minutes.

At school, she said little. None of her peers knew Alvina's mother was sick, because no one was interested.

And yet, every evening, she still came home and set the table with a place for her mother. She still checked to see if Mary's napkin was folded, if her cup was turned the right way. These were the rituals she clung to.

Because if Mary left, there would be nothing to hold her place in the world. And Alvina wasn't sure she'd know how to exist without someone who thought she mattered.

The next day at school, Miss Tuttle lingered near her desk after class, not kindly, not with warmth, but with that pinched expression she often wore when papers were poorly written, or shoes were too scuffed.

She held Alvina's essay as if it had offended her.

"This is your idea of a *home* essay?" she said, tapping the page. "It's all emotion. No structure. No clear argument."

Alvina kept her eyes down. "Yes, ma'am."

"The quiet in the house is the loudest thing I know," Miss Tuttle read aloud, sneering slightly. "What am I supposed to do with that? Are you writing poetry now?"

"No, ma'am."

Miss Tuttle clicked her tongue. "If you want higher marks, Alvina, I suggest you stick to facts next time. And leave the dramatics for church plays."

She dropped the essay on Alvina's desk and walked away without waiting for a response.

Alvina picked it up slowly, her fingers brushing over the red ink that bled across the page. *Too vague. Unclear. Off-topic.*

She folded the paper carefully and slid it between the pages of her reader, not because she needed to review it, but because she couldn't bear to throw it away. It was the only time she'd ever tried to explain what the silence felt like. And even that had been wrong.

She didn't cry. Not there. Not where anyone might see.

At night, she curled beneath the quilt her mother had made years ago, when scraps were precious and time was a kind of love. The corners didn't match, and some of the stitches bunched in crooked rows, but Alvina knew every patch by memory. This one was from Mary's old apron. That one from the hem of a dress she'd outgrown. It smelled faintly of cedar and starch, and Alvina pressed her face to it like it might still carry her mother's warmth.

Under her pillow, she kept a pair of Mary's socks, soft, faded wool, worn thin at the heels. She hadn't meant to keep them there. She'd found them balled up in the laundry basket the day after Mary went into the hospital and hadn't been able to put them away.

Some nights, when the house felt too quiet and the dark pressed too close, she'd slip them on her feet. They were sagging at the ankles. But they made her feel less hollow. Less forgotten.

She never told anyone about the socks. Not George. Not even Mary, when she visited and sat silently beside the hospital bed, her eyes searching for words she couldn't say.

It was a small thing. But it helped her sleep.

When she visited her mother after school, the lone nurse in charge of taking care of Mary always greeted her with a tired smile and a kind, soft voice. She was one of those women who lived on the outskirts of town, too far for many rumors to reach, and saw Mary and Alvina as the ailing mother and the worried daughter they were.

"She's resting today, but she's been asking for you," the nurse would say. "You can sit with her, try not to wake her."

Alvina would nod and clutch the strap of her book satchel tighter for support. The walk through the hospital hallway always felt endless, each step heavier than the last, the air too warm and too still.

But the silence at home was worse.

After school, the kitchen was quiet—no smell of broth simmering, no radio playing softly in the background. But boys were around making useless noise as always.

The only relief she had was sleep. But on the worst nights when even that refused to come, she crept barefoot through the dark hallway to her mother's rocking chair. She'd pull the pillow into her lap and press her face into it, the faint scent of lavender still clinging to the fabric. It made her throat close.

Sometimes she sat there for hours, holding it like it might hold her back.

I don't know how to do this, Mama, she'd think, blinking into the dark. *I can't keep pretending everything's fine.*

George visited Mary at the hospital, but only in the evening after work. His visits were short. He'd sit for a while in silence, maybe hold Mary's hand if she was awake, and then go. He rarely said much. But Alvina slowly noticed a change in him, too. His skin looked ashy, his cheeks hollow. He wasn't eating. His clothes hung loose, and he coughed when he didn't think anyone was watching. At first, she thought it was grief or exhaustion. But then came the chill in her gut. Something wasn't right with him either.

But Alvina didn't know how to bring something like that up to her father. They had never shared that kind of closeness, and so she resolved to bite her tongue whenever such thoughts came to mind. Still, the grief compounded as both her parents waned, physically and mentally, and sometimes Alvina grew stiff with terror at the prospect of both her parents passing before the year's end.

Weeks passed with Mary in the hospital. Sometimes Alvina would come in to find her propped up in a wooden chair by the window, her hands warm and full of life, her eyes dancing with affection.

"Did you bring the lemon candies?" she asked one afternoon with a tired smile.

Alvina grinned and pulled them from her coat pocket. "I saved the lemon one for you. The peppermint for me."

Mary's fingers trembled as she unwrapped the candy. "You're a good girl, Alvina. Too good."

But other days were silent. Mary would lie curled under the stiff white hospital blankets, her breathing thin and irregular. Alvina would sit beside her, watching the laborious rise and fall of her chest.

Back at home, everything fell on Alvina's shoulders. Without knowing it, George found himself giving Alvina every single one of Mary's old chores, on top of those she'd already had before. It was up to her now to scrub the floors until her back ached, and to keep the house from slipping into chaos. Homework was barely an afterthought. Her grades dropped.

A stinging strike on the wrist woke Alvina with a start.

"Alvina, that's the third time this week you've fallen asleep."

"I'm sorry, Miss Carter. It won't happen again."

"It better not."

But it did, several times that week as well as the next. Finally, after Miss Carter made her stand in the back of the classroom for an entire day as punishment for nodding off again, Alvina decided she'd had enough.

"Papa, I don't want to go back to school."

George looked up from his breakfast plate at a meal Alvina herself had cooked.

"What's that?"

"I said I'm not going back. I'll stay home. I'll take care of everything. The house, the laundry, cooking, and cleaning."

"Alvina, you know you can't do that. Not with how far you've gotten in school already."

"But I'm not learning anything there! I'm too tired to learn anything anymore – all my energy is taken up by taking care of the house. I've been doing everything at home!" Alvina cried, her voice shaking as tears welled in her eyes. "For weeks now! Mama is in the hospital, and you're gone all day. The boys don't even care; they won't help. They won't even *visit* her!"

George looked down at his calloused hands but said nothing. Alvina thought of all the times he'd stayed silent like this before, and her face grew hot with frustration years in the making.

"And I worry about you, too! Because you're sick as well. You don't eat. You don't help with the dishes or the laundry. You don't do anything!"

He rubbed the bridge of his nose and let out a long, tired breath. "Last night… your brothers and I talked. While you were at the hospital."

Alvina narrowed her eyes. "About what?"

He hesitated. "Things. Chores. The way things have been going."

Her voice was flat. "And?"

He looked up at her, eyes dull. "It's a mess. I know. But I think if we give it a little more time."

"Time?" she snapped. "Mama is in the hospital. The house is falling apart. Charles hasn't spoken a full sentence in days, and Henry acts like nothing matters."

"They're grieving."

"So am I!" she shouted. "But I still get up. I still cook. I still go to school and try to act normal while they sit in silence and wait for someone else to fix it."

George flinched but said nothing.

"You said you talked," she said bitterly. "Was there a plan, or more silence?"

His gaze dropped to the floor. "They're not ready. I… I didn't push it."

Alvina stared at him. "Of course not."

"Don't do that."

"Do what? Do you expect me to take care of your sons? To help?"

His voice rose, brittle and defensive. "I am helping. I go to work every day."

"So did she. And she still made dinner and folded our clothes and braided my hair in the morning."

He looked away.

The silence between them yawned wide. Alvina turned to the counter and made herself a sandwich with stale bread and a smear of jelly. Her hands trembled slightly as she cut it in half. She didn't look at him again.

She tucked her schoolbooks under one arm and walked to the door. Her hand hovered over the latch. She wanted to slam it. To rattle the walls. To scream something childish and awful and true.

But she didn't.

She opened it gently. Stepped outside. And let it close behind her with a soft, infuriating click.

Inside, no one followed her.

No one said a word.

That night, the kitchen was dark after dinner. The dishes stacked up. The pot sat crusted on the stove. No one offered to clean. No one offered anything.

Alvina walked past Charles and Henry in the hallway. They barely glanced at her.

She stood in the doorway of her bedroom, holding her books to her chest, feeling the weight of every unspoken word she'd swallowed since her mother fell ill.

They were all still breathing and still walking through the house. But she had never felt more alone.

But Mary wasn't recovering. Though the fever broke, her strength never returned. The doctors said the pneumonia had passed, but her heart had suffered. It struggled now with every beat.

One morning, George took the doctor aside in the hallway.

"She isn't coming home, is she?"

The doctor didn't sugarcoat it. "No, Mr. Williams. Her heart's too weak. I'm sorry."

Alvina spent every afternoon at the hospital, curled beside her mother on a narrow chair, her hands folded tightly in her lap until Mary stirred. The room carried the sharp tang of antiseptic mixed with the fading sweetness of wilting flowers, but Alvina tried to soften it with stories.

Mary's lips curved faintly as Alvina described Charles dropping the last slice of bread, only for the family dog to snatch it up before it touched the floor. "That old dog," Mary murmured, her eyes warming with amusement. "Always quicker than Charles." Alvina chuckled, leaning closer. "Smarter than him, too."

Mary's hand trembled as she lifted it, brushing her daughter's cheek with a touch light as paper. "You're going to be all right," she whispered. Alvina blinked back tears, summoning a smile.

"You'll be home soon, Mama. We'll sit on the porch and watch the garden bloom again." Mary looked at her with that quiet, weary love that spoke louder than words. "Take care of yourself," she said softly. "You're stronger than you think."

Later that afternoon, Mary drifted into sleep. Her breathing grew shallow, her face peaceful in a way that unsettled Alvina. A nurse slipped inside, gently lowering the back of the bed, and gave Alvina a tender and compassionate look. "Stretch your legs for a bit, dear," the nurse suggested.

Hesitant, Alvina rose and stepped into the hallway. Her shoes echoed against the polished floor as she walked slowly, whispering prayers she dared not speak aloud. She was gone only a few minutes, but when she returned, the room felt changed.

Her mother was still. No breath. No motion. The stillness pressed against the walls like a heavy fog.

"Mama?" Alvina's voice cracked as she moved closer, hope clinging stubbornly to each step. The nurse appeared at her side, quiet like a shadow, and laid a gentle hand on her shoulder. "Her heart stopped," she said softly. "She didn't feel a thing."

The words emptied the room of sound.

Alvina sank into the chair, gathering her mother's hand between her own as if she could coax warmth back into the fingers. "No… Mama… please don't go." Her whisper broke into sobs.

She bent low, pressing her face into the quilt, inhaling the faint trace of lavender soap that lingered in the fabric. Her tears seeped into the worn patchwork, her shoulders trembling with grief.

For a long time, she wept, her broken whispers filling the silence. "I can't do this without you. I don't know how."

The nurse lingered close but let her grieve, the ticking of the hallway clock marking time in a world that carried on, indifferent to the fact that Mary was gone.

Chapter 4

By the time Alvina finished high school, she had blossomed, or at least, that's how others saw it. Her posture was straighter, her voice more assured, and the quiet shyness that had once defined her began to lift. But inside, Alvina still carried a shadow. She had grown up in a home that never quite felt like hers, one stitched together from two broken families. After her mother died when Alvina was fifteen, silence filled the corners of the house. Her stepfather never quite took to her, and most days, Alvina felt like a stranger rather than a daughter.

She rarely invited friends over, too aware of the tension that lingered in her home. Still, by her senior year she had managed to gather a small circle of girls—classmates who sat with her at lunch, swapped notes before exams, and sometimes lingered with her after school. They weren't inseparable, but they gave her the comfort of being included, of laughter shared in hallways and whispered secrets that made her feel, at least for a while, like she belonged.

So, when George quietly arranged a part-time job for her at the Catholic Church office during her last two years of high school, it was more than work; it was a lifeline.

"She needs a little encouragement," George had told Father Dugan, his hat twisting in his hands. "She's got the brains but needs someone to believe in her."

"She has my vote," the priest had replied without hesitation.

Typing bulletins, filing forms, and addressing parish mail gave Alvina structure and purpose. It was work she could count on, a rhythm that quieted the hollow spaces in her life. More than that, it gave her a place where no one looked at her like she was a leftover from another family. At the church office, she was simply *Alvina who could be counted on.*

Still, after graduation, the long summer evenings stretched out before her like unanswered questions. She lingered at the edge of gatherings, smiling politely, unsure where she fit. It was Marcie who first tugged her in.

"Come on, Alvina," Marcie said one afternoon as they walked home from school for the last time, her books tucked under one arm. "You can't spend the whole summer in that parish office. You'll turn into a filing cabinet."

Ruth giggled, looping her arm through Alvina's. "We're going to Indianapolis. Just for a look. Jobs, maybe. You should come."

Hazel nodded, her grin wide. "We'll be grown-ups then. Think of it—we'll have paychecks, rooms of our own, maybe even new dresses that *aren't* hand-me-downs."

Alvina hesitated. She had learned not to expect much, not to plan too far ahead. These girls had siblings and noisy, loving homes. They laughed easily and talked about futures as if they had always expected one. For Alvina, futures had always seemed borrowed, fragile, one accident away from slipping through her fingers.

But their enthusiasm was contagious.

"Well…" she began, her voice cautious. "I suppose it wouldn't hurt to look."

"Not just look," Marcie declared. "We're doing this. The four of us. You'll see."

And for once, Alvina said yes.

They spent weeks in whispered conversations, huddled in the corner of the diner with pencils scratching over scraps of paper. They scribbled out bus fares, cheap hotel rates, the cost of meals if they shared plates. They pooled their babysitting money, wages from part-time jobs, and Christmas envelopes that had been carefully tucked away.

When the day finally came, they packed modest suitcases with sturdy shoes and dresses that could be worn twice in the same week without notice. At the Greyhound station, the scent of diesel and hot pavement mingled with the thrum of their nerves.

"Front seats or back?" Hazel asked, clutching her ticket like a lifeline.

"Back," Ruth answered. "More fun back there."

Marcie elbowed to Alvina playfully. "This is it—our first step into the world."

Alvina smiled shyly, gripping the handle of her worn valise. As the bus doors hissed open, she followed them up the steps. Their excitement filled the space between their seats like electricity, and for the first time in a long while, Alvina felt as though she was part of something beginning.

She and three girls from school, Marcie, Ruth, and Hazel, decided to visit Indianapolis to scout for jobs. Alvina hesitated at first. These girls had siblings and noisy, loving homes. They laughed easily and talked about futures as if they had always expected one. Alvina had learned not to expect much.

Still, she said yes.

"I brought my lucky penny," Ruth said, grinning. "Found it heads-up outside the drugstore."

"I brought extra stockings," Marcie added. "In case Hazel spills coffee again."

"I don't spill coffee," Hazel retorted.

Alvina sat by the window, her hands folded tightly in her lap. She watched the familiar farmland slide away and wondered if the city would feel like home.

They arrived at a hum of trolley bells and endless sidewalks.

"Look at all these buildings," Marcie whispered. "We're not in Jasper anymore."

For three days, they explored. They stepped carefully around puddles, peeked into shop windows, and wrote down addresses from bulletin boards and newspaper classifieds. Most of the work they found was for waitresses or shopgirls. The kind of work Alvina feared might be filled with too much chatter and not enough corners to hide in.

Then, on the third morning, as they rounded the corner of a quiet street, Alvina spotted a typed sign taped to a glass-paneled office door:

"Typist Wanted – Inquire on the 3rd Floor."

She pointed quickly. "Girls," she said, tugging Ruth's sleeve, "This might be it."

They climbed the narrow staircase, which smelled of varnish and sweat. At the top, a man in wire-rimmed glasses looked up from behind a desk.

"You here for the typing pool?"

"Yes, sir," Hazel answered, smoothing her skirt.

"All four of you?"

Alvina hesitated. Four felt like too many. What if they laughed at her? What if she wasn't good enough?

"We can type sixty words a minute," she said anyway, finding her voice.

The man raised his eyebrows. "Well then. We're starting a new freight company. Interviews are brief. We need smart, focused girls."

He watched each of them fill out forms, his eyes moving quickly between their names and their penmanship. Alvina's hands shook slightly, but her letters were even. She had practiced them again, late at night by lamplight, alone in her room.

By the end of the hour, three of them were offered jobs. Ruth declined, choosing instead to return home. Her family needed her, she said. Alvina wondered what that felt like to be required.

That evening, they returned to a clean white boardinghouse they'd admired earlier. It had polished floors and rooms with individual sinks. The restrooms were down the hall, but the price was fair, and the landlady, Mrs. Bonner, was firm but kind.

"I don't allow foolishness under my roof," she told them, her sharp eyes scanning their faces. "But I do expect ambition."

Alvina gave the slightest nod, grateful for the chance to be measured by what she could do, not by where she came from.

They signed the lease with nervous smiles.

As the bus rolled out of the city the next morning, headed back to Jasper to pack their things, Alvina sat by the window. Her heartbeat is fast.

"We're doing this," Marcie said.

"Yes," Alvina replied, fingers wrapped around the worn leather handle of her handbag. "This is our beginning."

Three weeks later, after long days of typing invoices and filing documents, after countless awkward hallway greetings with strangers and learning how to tune out city sirens at night, the girls needed something lighter.

One warm evening, as they walked home under a sky that smelled faintly of summer rain and hot pavement, Hazel grinned and pulled a flyer from her pocket.

"Look what I found on the bulletin board at church."

Marcie narrowed her eyes. "A sermon?"

Hazel laughed. "Close. A dance. This Friday night at the parish hall. It says, *'Young Adult Social – Music and Refreshments – All Are Welcome.'* We should go."

Marcie wrinkled her nose. "Sounds like lemonade and long faces."

"I'm serious," Hazel said. "We haven't met anyone. Just coworkers and Mrs. Bonner's cat. It's time."

"I don't know," Alvina murmured, slowing her steps. "I've never been to something like that."

Hazel turned, surprised. "You've never been to a dance?"

"Not really. There was one at school once, but I didn't stay long. I… I never knew how to fit in." She gave a slight, embarrassing shrug. "I didn't grow up like you girls."

Hazel's teasing softened. "Well, you do now. You belong to us. And we're going."

Marcie reached over and squeezed Alvina's arm. "You'll have a good time. You need to wear that blue dress and smile at someone cute."

Alvina laughed, though it caught in her throat. "Do I have to smile at anyone?"

"Only if you want to," Hazel winked.

"Alright," Alvina said after a pause, her voice small but steady. "Let's go."

She wasn't sure if she could dance like the others or talk to boys without fumbling over her words. But she had crossed so many thresholds already, what was one more?

And maybe, just maybe, this next one would feel like a step toward something more than a beginning.

On Friday, as soon as the office clock struck five, the three women nearly flew out the door. They shared a quick meal of soup and biscuits in the downstairs dining room of the boardinghouse, barely touching their food before dashing upstairs. The next hour, there was a whirlwind of curling irons heating on the vanity, borrowed lipstick shades, and trial-and-error with bobby pins.

"Hazel, turn so I can fix your collar," Alvina said, smoothing the navy fabric. "You look like you're about to lead a Navy parade."

Marcie laughed from the corner. "Well, I'm wearing my lucky stockings. If we don't meet any gentlemen tonight, it's not for lack of trying."

By the time they stepped out onto the sidewalk, they were glowing with anticipation. The church was only three blocks away, the sidewalks still warm from the late sun, their shoes clicking in unison as they walked.

The church's community room had been transformed. Paper lanterns hung from the rafters, casting soft golden light over the hall. A four-piece band, accordion, trumpet, piano, and fiddle, was tuning up on the small stage. The scent of lemon punch and waxed floors floated in the air, mingling with murmurs of conversation and bursts of laughter.

Alvina paused at the doorway; her hands clutched tightly around her small purse. She'd never seen a room so full of motion, light, and unfamiliar faces.

"This is prettier than I expected," she said softly, trying to sound at ease.

Hazel grinned. "And look, actual gentlemen. Not a single farm boy in overalls."

Alvina smiled back but said nothing. Her mouth was dry.

They paid their fifteen-cent admission fee and stepped into the room. Tables lined the walls, topped with gingham linens and flickering candles set inside Mason jars. The dance floor was already filling, women smoothing their skirts and men tugging nervously at their collars.

Alvina stood stiffly beside her friends, eyes darting across the room. Every laugh sounded louder than it was. Every woman seemed more graceful, more certain of her place.

"Relax," Hazel whispered, elbowing her gently. "You look fine."

"I feel like I'm wearing my shoes on the wrong feet."

"Don't look down."

When the music began, Marcie was the first to be asked to dance, followed quickly by Hazel. Alvina smiled and nodded as they were whisked away, but she stayed near the wall, pretending to examine the fabric of the tablecloth beside her.

After a few minutes, a tall man with a confident smile approached. "Care to dance?"

"Oh yes," she said, a beat too late. She stumbled slightly as she stepped forward, bumping her hip onto the edge of the table.

He chuckled politely and offered his arm.

He said his name was Jack. He worked in a bakery and had flour permanently lodged under his fingernails. He led well, but Alvina's feet were too tight in her shoes, and she had to keep reminding herself to breathe. She tried to make conversation, but her mind went blank.

"Do you like music?" he asked.

"Yes."

"What kind?"

"Um... I'm not sure. The kind with words?" she said, immediately regretting it.

Jack smiled kindly. "That's most music, I suppose."

He was gracious enough not to press further, but Alvina winced inwardly and resolved not to speak unless spoken to.

Her second partner was a shorter man with wire-rimmed glasses and nervous energy. He taught at the elementary school and asked her what she did for work. She managed to explain about the freight office but lost her train of thought halfway through and had to start again.

He nodded, perhaps more out of politeness than interest.

By the third dance, she was ready to sit out the rest of the night. Her face burned from the effort of smiling, and her underarms felt damp despite the cool air in the room.

Then a quiet voice broke through her fog.

"Would you like to dance?"

She turned to see a slightly shy man with light brown hair and a kind, open face. His posture wasn't too stiff, nor too bold, and he had enough confidence to ask, and enough gentleness to wait.

"I... I would," she said, her voice uncertain.

They stepped onto the dance floor. He offered his hand without presumption, and she placed hers in his. His touch was warm but not sweaty. He counted softly as they moved, helping her stay with the rhythm.

"I'm Lawrence. Lawrence Hursting."

"Alvina Williams," she replied, barely meeting his eyes. "You're good at this."

He smiled. "My sisters made sure of that. We weren't allowed to stand on the sidelines at weddings."

She chuckled, grateful for the pause in pressure.

They danced for a few more turns. Lawrence didn't pepper her with questions, which was a relief. When he did speak, it was in simple, thoughtful phrases. He asked where she was from, and she answered carefully, avoiding mentioning her complicated family.

When he asked what books she liked, she hesitated. "I read mostly... practical things. Cookbooks. Church pamphlets."

He repeated with a smile. "You must be a good cook then."

She wrinkled her nose. "Not really. Just curious, I guess."

He nodded, like that was more than enough.

As the evening wore on, they danced again. The second time, she felt more relaxed until he twirled her unexpectedly, and she bumped into a passing couple.

"Oh! I'm so sorry," she gasped, clutching his shoulder.

"You're fine," Lawrence said gently, steadying her with one hand. "It's a dance floor, not a parade ground."

Alvina laughed, half with relief, half with embarrassment. "I think I'm more used to typewriter keys than music notes."

He leaned in slightly. "You're doing fine."

By the time the band announced its final song, her cheeks were flushed not from dancing, but from something quieter, warmer.

At the refreshment table, he poured a cup of punch for her. They stood side by side, not speaking for a moment.

"I hope you'll come to the next one," he said at last, his voice quieter than before.

"I will," she replied, her hand tightening on the cup. "And I hope you'll save me a dance."

He smiled, tucking his hands into his pockets. "I'll save you two dances."

Alvina sipped her punch and looked down at her shoes. They still pinched. But they were pointing forward now.

Chapter 5

Alvina left the first dance feeling flushed with excitement. As she walked home, her feet throbbed inside stiff, narrow shoes. Each step would've been its agony, on another night.

"I feel like I'm floating," Alvina said.

"That's because you're walking on blisters."

Still, Alvina grinned.

"I am going to buy new dancing shoes," she declared. "More comfortable ones, but not cheap ones, either. I'll have to get them sometime soon, too, if I'm going next Friday. Hazel, do you know what stores sell dancing shoes?"

Marcie snorted. "You're planning next Friday already?"

"I don't see the harm," Alvina said, a bit defensively.

"I do. There were a couple of men there, you probably didn't see them, Alvina, since you weren't on the dance floor too much, but they were handsy whenever I danced with them. Now, if anything, I'm not a prude, but at some point…"

Hazel's voice soon sounded as though it were two blocks away from Alvina. She had begun to slip off into her reveries, a mixture of recalling the slightest details of the past few hours and imagining the most vivid portrait of how next Friday might go. So it was that she went to bed that night without even wishing her roommates good night, too preoccupied to slip off anything more than the tight shoes before falling asleep atop the covers. It wasn't until the next morning that Alvina remembered the tear in her dress.

Alvina had barely sat down for breakfast before Hazel leaned across the table.

"What's his name?"

Her face grew hot, and then hotter still when she tried to recompose herself.

"I don't know what you're talking about."

"Alvina, please. I saw you sitting with him all night. It's no use trying to play dumb."

Surprisingly, being detected relieved Alvina. Though she would've never brought the matter up herself, she wanted to talk about the night before a good deal.

"Lawrence. Lawrence Hursting."

"Did you like him?"

"I think he'd make a good husband, if that's what you mean."

Hazel raised her hand like a traffic cop.

"Slow down. Alvina, you met him at one dance. One. Let's keep the wedding bells on hold."

But wasn't that what you talked to boys your age for? To see how compatible you were. Alvina might've spoken such thoughts if she had been less aware of how little she knew of men and talking to them.

"You didn't date in high school, did you?" Hazel asked. Alvina shook her head.

"Well, don't go grabbing the first apple on the tree and expect it to be sweet. I mean, he *is* cute," Hazel said. "At least, from what I saw of him from afar. But throwing that word around, *husband*, is a bit much. I mean, how much can you learn about someone in one night?"

"I wasn't, I mean, I'm not, I liked talking to him."

"You did glow all the way home," Marcie said with a grin as she passed through the kitchen.

"Try dancing with a few other men next time, just to see," Hazel said.

Alvina nodded politely, but a feeling of frustration was all that had come from her friends' advice. They didn't know what it felt like to grow up surrounded by half-brothers who treated her like a maid or what it meant to miss out on every school dance. Last night, she had felt seen. What could be wrong with that? Still, she felt obligated to take the idea of meeting more people to heart. She knew Hazel meant well and was speaking from a place of far more experience than herself, too.

The ensuing week passed in a single mood of anticipation, interrupted only by sleep. Marcie and Hazel agreed to go to JCPenney's after church that Sunday to help Alvina shop for shoes and ended up helping her pick out her first lipstick and bottle of perfume in the process. The shopping itself embarrassed Alvina, who felt the activity perfectly displayed the extent of her naiveté regarding all things feminine. But she was more than pleased with the result, and by Monday night, she had already begun to arrange the more minute details of what outfit she would wear and how she'd do her makeup for the next dance.

By Thursday, her excitement was almost unbearable. The blue-and-white striped blouse and a navy skirt she'd picked out at the beginning of the week hung eagerly on the only metal hanger Alvina had. Her new black shoes gleamed beneath a pair of crisp white ankle socks. Even her hairpins were neatly arranged on the dresser, the same six she'd used the previous week, sitting primly parallel beside one another.

All week, the thought of putting on the outfit had tempted her unsuccessfully. "I'll have to iron the blouse all over again," she told herself whenever the thought reemerged. But it was less than an hour after coming home from work that Thursday when the outfit finally came off its special hanger.

Alvina was gauging how the belt suited her waist when the sound of a voice made her jump.

"You're going to flutter over Lawrence the whole night again?" Marcie asked with a grin. "If only he knew how much you were doing for him."

Alvina blushed.

"You could've knocked. And I was only putting it on to make sure it fit."

"At least let another boy *see* you this time."

"I danced with two other men last time. Why do you and Hazel keep acting like I didn't?"

"Because you didn't hide away with them for nearly two hours while the rest of us were dancing."

Alvina decided it would be best to ignore Marcie and began smoothing out her outfit as though she were alone in the room.

"Ten bucks says Hazel wants to scope out new arrivals," Marcie said. Alvina kept smoothing out the skirt.

"Well, don't get mad at me if he's not everything you remember him as."

She slipped out the door as quietly as she'd come in. Alvina sighed but soon forgot about the conversation entirely and sneaked into the bathroom to try and better gauge how she looked.

Friday passed quickly enough, and the three girls arrived at the church well before the dance was fully set up. Hazel complained about not having enough time to get ready. Then Marcie complained that they were walking too fast, so that her dress shoes were hurting her feet. Alvina pressed on without a second thought.

Her determination was quickly rewarded. No less than a few seconds after paying her entry fee, Alvina quickly spotted Lawrence. He had gotten there even earlier than the girls, as he was helping set-up chairs and straighten the gingham tablecloths when Alvina spotted him.

Lawrence caught her gaze at him before she could look away, and it was difficult for her to look him in the eyes as he came up to her and began speaking.

"Hi, Alvina," he said, walking over. "You look wonderful."

"Thank you," she replied, her voice catching slightly. "I like your tie."

"I ironed it myself," he joked. "Want to help me finish setting up the rest of the tablecloths?"

As the band tuned up, the two others sat at a table on the other side of the dance floor, watching Alvina and Lawrence from afar.

"Is he *ever* going to let her breathe?" Hazel said.

"He hasn't left her side since we got here," Marcie said.

It had been fifteen minutes since their arrival.

"I thought she said she was going to meet other guys tonight," Hazel said.

"But did you believe her when she said that?"

Hazel sighed.

"I at least thought she'd pretend to. So much for that."

"I bet you they don't leave each other's side the whole night."

Indeed, it took nearly two hours for the young man and woman to separate. Lawrence asked her to dance almost every song, and she said yes, every time. He was an even better dancer than she had imagined, and she found herself making an impressive figure simply by following his lead well enough. He didn't crowd her, but he didn't drift far, either. It was only when Lawrence volunteered to get Alvina some punch that they finally separated for all of thirty seconds.

"Do you have plans tomorrow?" Lawrence asked as he returned.

"No, I don't think so."

"Would you want to go on a picnic with me?"

The next morning, Lawrence arrived at the agreed-upon time down to the minute. The landlady let Alvina know a visitor had arrived, and Alvina went down the stairs in a pale-yellow blouse and a skirt that brushed her knees. Her hair was braided and pinned.

She found Lawrence sitting stiffly in the parlor. When he saw her, he smiled and stood. "Did you pack the lunch?"

Her smile vanished.

"No," she said, trying to keep her tone light. "I figured we'd stop at the store and grab sandwiches."

"Oh," was all Lawrence said. He pursed and unpursued his lips, and it was up to Alvina to take the lead and suggest a nearby store they could walk to get bread and meat for sandwiches.

She forced a polite smile as they walked, but she couldn't bring herself to speak. She thought she could discern a touch of disappointment in Lawrence's face as they walked.

If you invite someone on a picnic, you bring the food," she thought to herself irritably. *"I should've said, 'Why didn't you pack the lunch?' You can't expect me to plan it like a servant."*

Her older brothers' voices echoed in her mind

"Set the table, Alvina."

"Why isn't dinner ready?"

"Can you make food any slower?"

The frustration and shame of years of being treated like a maid in her own house rose to the surface. So it was that, as the two shopped for an impromptu meal, Alvina came to recognize the scales of measurement she'd used to judge Lawrence thus far. He'd passed the first few tests with such grace that she'd assumed he would ace them all without fail. But the frustration and shame of years of being treated like a maid in her own house rose again, as she said otherwise. For the first time since they'd sat down at the dance they'd met at, the image Alvina had carved out for Lawrence fell flat against the man who now asked her which bread to choose. His tone grated on her as they shopped as well; though she'd always thought it the embodiment of confidence, it came off as conceited now, and she couldn't help but feel that his nose and ears were not as proportionate as they should've been, either.

The bleeding finally stopped when Lawrence insisted on paying the moment they grabbed the last ingredient. Walking to the park also furthered his cause, as Alvina appreciated the latent athleticism of his gait and the neatness of his outfit. He had at least taken to heart dressing up for the occasion.

At the park, he produced a blanket from the car and laid it out beneath a tree.

"This spot, okay?" he asked.

She nodded, still trying to soften what lingered of her initial disappointment. "It's perfect."

They spent the afternoon in quiet conversation, talking about music, food, and childhood pets. That day, more than their previous two meetings, Alvina realized how easily Lawrence could make her laugh; she also appreciated the fact that when she spoke, he always listened well. An uncontrollable smile would come over her whenever he mentioned this or that small detail she'd said an hour ago, a week ago, or when they first met.

By the time Lawrence said goodbye to her at the front door of her apartment, she had forgiven the lunch oversight. But she had not forgotten it, and as she undressed and prepared for bed, Alvina did not play back the bright moments of her time with Lawrence as she had done after their previous two meetings.

Chapter 6

A few other dates followed their picnic, during which Alvina's scales of favor and ambivalence for Lawrence rose and fell several times. She found herself at her happiest when they were dancing together, and nearly at her happiest during those conversations that came in between and immediately after dancing. It was then that Lawrence seemed to be his happy, eloquent, and considerate self.

"If only we were always dancing," Alvina sometimes thought to herself.

Indeed, she looked forward to the Friday night dances, which they both now went to without fail, much more than their other dates. Outside the dance hall, Alvina found Lawrence's attentiveness often lapsed when she felt it was most needed, and that his cheerful confidence, which impressed on the dance floor, could come off as impersonal and even condescending outside of it.

Still, Alvina felt the scales leaned in his favor well enough. She tried to please him whenever possible and remembered many of his compliments weeks after they were given. So too could she recall each act of service he dealt with after a date, and she'd usually tally them up in his favor that night while lying in her bed.

But what she did not tally up, and what might've been the most significant swing in Lawrence's favor, was the escape from loneliness he provided to Alvina. Even on their worst dates, Alvina found herself confiding more in all the things she'd never been to say to anyone else besides her mother. She liked to lean against him sometimes when they walked, so that his presence would help boost her up rather than let her fall, and even when he wasn't with her, the mere thought of him could usually give Alvina a comfort she'd thought unrecoverable once her mother had died. So, it was eight weeks after that first dance.

As the Great War raged on in early 1917, the church's Friday evening social grew quieter with each passing week. More men were drafted each week, in addition to those enlisting voluntarily, so the parish committee scaled back the gatherings to once a month.

Three weeks separated the last weekly dance from the first monthly one, so that the only Friday night dance in April brought together Alvina and Lawrence once more for the first time in over two weeks. The two danced phenomenally but were a bit awkward with one another during the church dinner of stewed beef and buttered rolls, and as they walked together under the gas lamps toward the streetcar stop, Alvina found she had nothing to say to Lawrence. It felt as though the city itself was tongue-tied in its way. A hush had fallen over Indianapolis since the war began, and Alvina realized with surprise that she could hear their footsteps smacking on the concrete as they walked onwards. Lawrence stopped before they reached the corner.

"Alvina," he began, his voice gentler than usual, "would you be free Sunday afternoon? I'd like you to come to my parents' house for dinner."

Alvina blinked. Having learned during their picnic that Lawrence's parents lived only a short distance from her boardinghouse, Alvina had been wondering when this invitation might come for a little while now.

"Yes," she said, with a smile she hoped would mask her sudden nerves. "Of course. I'd be honored."

"They're sweet, I promise," he added, as if trying to make it sound less imposing. "Just my folks and my sister. It'll be a quiet meal. I'll pick you up around six?"

"Sounds great."

Over the next day and a half, Alvina's train of thought strayed little from what she was to wear for that Sunday dinner. Her wardrobe had expanded since she started to work, but choosing the right outfit still felt daunting.

Friday evening, she pulled out several combinations and laid them on the bed. She still hadn't decided on what to wear yet, having drawn up and scrapped about a dozen outfits since getting home from work.

A noise in the hallway alerted Alvina to two peeping pairs of eyes, who soon joined Alvina in her room to discuss what she was to wear. In the end, Marcie and Hazel helped Alvina settle on a navy skirt paired with a pale pink blouse, along with flat navy shoes and a small matching purse.

Then on Sunday, Hazel insisted on doing Alvina's hair by twisting the long strands into a braided crown, pinned with two silver clips that caught the light. A dab of rouge and powder, a careful curl to her lashes, and a faint rose-scented perfume completed the transformation. Alvina thanked her lucky stars she hadn't waited until Sunday to lay out her dressing options. She had less than five minutes to spare before Hazel and Marcie were finally finished preparing her.

When Lawrence came to pick her up, Alvina's nerves returned in full force. She was surprised that he was walking, but she remembered that he said he lived close by. As they approached the walk up to the Hursting home, she saw the broad, two-story house trimmed in white and forest green, with a wraparound porch and a neatly tended yard of tulips and hydrangeas. It stood in stark contrast with the surrounding grey city apartments.

Mr. Hursting, Lawrence's father, greeted them at the door.

"Come on in," he said as he stepped aside. "We've been looking forward to meeting you."

Alvina smiled, nodded, and walked into the house in the most proper and polite gait she could manage. The house's interior was filled with polished wood, framed photographs, and delicate China displays. It smelled faintly of lemon oil and chicken dumplings.

Lawrence's mother greeted her briefly, hands already full with serving spoons.

"You must be Alvina. Sit, sit. Dinner's nearly ready."

As she sat at the dinner table, Lawrence's father reemerged from the front hall. He, too, sat down, extending his hand as he did so.

"Frank Hursting. I hear you work for the new freight company?"

"I do, sir. I'm a typing clerk," she said, straightening her shoulders. "I started this past spring."

He nodded with an expression Alvina found unreadable.

"Mm. A good, steady job, I suppose."

All Alvina could think of doing was nodding and smiling. She began to wonder if the whole evening would be like this.

The dining room table was already set with delicate porcelain dishes and silverware when Alvina arrived. She complimented the cups out of politeness, to which Lawrence's father responded curtly.

"Don't know anything about dishes."

A few minutes of stiff silence followed, and it was no small wave of relief that washed over her when Lawrence emerged from the kitchen, where he'd been talking to his mother, and joined the two at the table. He did his best to lead the conversation about the weather and the sale of war bonds downtown. His father shifted easily into topics of business and current events. With careful restraint, Alvina answered with his polite inquiries about her hometown, her family, and her work.

"My mother passed away when I was fifteen," she said quietly. "I have two older brothers and my stepfather in Jasper. I came to Indianapolis for a fresh start."

She avoided any mention of the tunnel house or the poverty she'd grown up in, as well as her older stepbrothers and how they treated her. Even Lawrence didn't know about that chapter of her life yet.

The meal of chicken dumplings, buttered peas, and warm cornbread was familiar and delicious. Alvina thanked Lawrence's mother lengthily and sipped her glass of white wine cautiously, unsure if it was proper to accept more than one pour.

Mrs. Hursting said little throughout dinner, rising frequently from the table to retrieve dishes or refill glasses without comment. She didn't ask Alvina more than one or two questions. In comparison, Cora, Lawrence's teenage sister, seemed friendlier and more talkative. Alvina felt she was much like her brother in some ways and enjoyed listening to her chatter about high school.

"I'm thinking of enrolling in secretarial school after graduation," she said at one point. Alvina noticed her father frowning at this comment.

"Nonsense. You'll do nothing of the kind."

"I don't think it would hurt for her to go," Lawrence said.

"Well, I do," his father said in such a way that it almost scared Alvina to hear.

"But Dad…"

"We'll talk about this later," he interrupted with a solemn finality. Cora flushed and excused herself from the dinner. Alvina expected her mother to follow the girl out – Cora looked close to crying when she left the table – but the woman watched her husband in mild anticipation.

Alvina swallowed hard. Moments earlier, she had finished explaining her job, and now the air felt thick with disapproval of something the same. Would Mr. Hursting have dismissed her like that if she had been in Cora's place? Such thoughts haunted Alvina throughout the rest of the dinner, to the point that she couldn't shake the feeling she had been filled away as a girl from the working class, practical, perhaps, but not suitable for their son.

After dinner, Mr. Hursting gestured. "Let's move outside. The air is fine tonight. Make us some tea and bring it to us on the porch."

Alvina moved towards the kitchen to help as the two men stepped outside, but Mrs. Hursting quickly waved her off. "Our guests don't lift a finger in this house," she said curtly.

As such, Alvina lagged behind the two men in coming out onto the porch, who were already firmly seated by the time she creaked open the door leading to the porch.

Though it was too dark to tell for sure, Alvina thought she saw Lawrence's father sit more upright and crane his neck ever so lightly when she came outside and sat beside Lawrence.

"Your mother is sweet," Alvina said to Lawrence, trying to cut the thick silence that had begun the moment she came out to join the pair.

"She is certainly good at what she does," said Lawrence's father, taking a puff of his cigar. "And what she does is very important."

Little else was said in the next few minutes, and it was with relief that Alvina saw Cora come outside, expertly balancing three pieces of cobbler as she did so. She was followed by her mother, who was likewise carrying a full load – a kettle of tea, a few teacups, and a handful of napkins – with an ease Alvina felt she could never replicate on her own.

But as soon as the two women came out and distributed what they held, they filed back inside, where Alvina saw them sit and poured their tea through the porch window. A chill deeper than the evening breeze came over Alvina.

Lawrence chatted easily with his father, unaware of the growing weight pressing on Alvina's shoulders. She sat politely on the porch swing, her tea growing cold in her hands, trying to hold her posture as her mind spiraled.

When Lawrence's father got up to use the restroom, Lawrence curled his arm tight around Alvina's nearby waist. She could see his cheerful smile through the fading twilight.

"They liked you. You did fine."

Alvina nodded; lips pressed into a smile that didn't reach her eyes. *Did fine* in her head. Was she supposed to have done better? Fine enough for a businessman's son? Fine enough to be tolerated, or to be invited back sometime soon?

Inside, she could still hear the soft clink of dishes and low voices; Mrs. Hursting and Cora were now scrubbing away in the kitchen. Steps came and went, and soon she heard Lawrence's father talking in a lowered voice that made her shiver uncontrollably. She took a slow sip of tea, hoping the warmth would distract her. But much loomed heavy in her chest throughout the rest of the night.

Lawrence insisted on walking her back to the boardinghouse once the night was up. The streets were quiet now, the only discernible sounds being the faint rattle of a distant streetcar and the muffled bark of a dog in some distant backyard. The evening air was crisp with the scent of lilacs and early spring.

He held her hand tightly, more firmly than usual, swinging it slightly as he talked.

"I think it went well," he said, almost giddy. "My father kept saying afterward that you're 'a well-spoken girl with a clear head.' That's high praise from him, believe me. And my mother loved you."

"I don't think we said more than ten words to each other," Alvina wanted to say to Lawrence, but she bit her tongue and instead offered a quiet laugh. Lawrence went on.

"Cora liked you, too. She's not much of a talker with strangers, but she didn't stop smiling after you asked about her school plans. That meant something."

Alvina nodded slowly.

"I'm glad," she said.

She wanted to ask: *Did your mother say anything about my job? Did your father frown when I mentioned boardinghouses?* But she continued to bite her tongue. None of the questions would form properly in her mouth. They all felt too sharp, too vulnerable.

By the time they reached the front steps of the boardinghouse, the porch light cast a warm halo over the door. Lawrence stopped at the first step and turned toward her. He took her hands in his and held them gently, then leaned in closer. "I love you, Alvina."

Then he kissed her softly, yet fully. His hands held hers still, as if he didn't want her to drift away. The street was quiet, the curtains in the boardinghouse still. Time stilled, too, for a moment. Before she could speak, Lawrence began again.

"Thank you for coming tonight. It meant a lot. My father liked you, and – well – my mother's always hard to read. But that's her way, always rushing about, focused on being the perfect host. You'll get used to it. I promise."

Alvina forced a smile.

"Thank you, Lawrence," she said. It was all she could manage in that moment; gratitude wrapped around a thousand complicated thoughts she couldn't untangle yet. She tried to tell the other thing she meant to say, that she wanted to say, but soon Lawrence began talking again, and by the time they said goodbye, the moment had passed.

As she walked into the boardinghouse, Marcie and Hazel nearly tackled Alvina onto the living room couch.

"We saw it! That kiss! We were watching through the sheer curtain!"

Hazel laughed, clutching a pillow to her chest.

"Was that your first kiss? Because, let me tell you, that was a *long* kiss. I don't know if I've ever seen one like that."

"I thought you did well," Marcie added, "very professional."

Alvina blushed, smoothing her skirt as she sat up. "You're both terrible." But she was smiling despite herself.

"Oh, quit it. We're wonderful and you know it. Who else would've spent their whole evening dressing you up like we did?"

"I think we are at least owed a summary of the night for our services," Marcie joked. "Tell us, what were his parents like? Don't hold back, either."

Alvina got up.

"Let me process the past few hours before I tell you about everything," she said, her voice more thoughtful than annoyed.

"Oh, c'mon, at least give us *something,* " Hazel whined. Guilt crept over Alvina.

"Well, his parents' home is close by. It's large and beautiful. Impeccably clean. It looks like something from a magazine on the outside... and it's even more formal on the inside."

The girls went quiet for a beat.

"That sounds intimidating," Marcie said.

"It was."

Then, with a tired smile, she assured her friends she'd tell them more the next day and climbed the stairs to her room. As she began her nighttime routine, her mind was still filled with gleaming porcelain dishes, stiff napkins, silver trays, and the feel of her hand swaying in Lawrence's as they walked home under the glow of the streetlights.

Later that night, Alvina sat on the edge of her narrow bed. The boardinghouse was nearly quiet, the only exception being the occasional creak of the old wood settling beneath the weight of some new sleeper in another nearby room. A moonbeam slipped between the curtains and stretched across the floor, pale and ghostly. She unlaced her shoes slowly, then pulled her legs beneath the quilt Hazel had lent her last winter.

She lay back, hands folded over her stomach, staring up at the ceiling. Her hair was still pinned up from dinner; she hadn't the heart to undo the braids. They felt like armor.

Alvina began to pray aloud, though for what she knew not. In time, she found that she wasn't praying at all. She was whispering into the dark. Not to God, but someone else.

"I know you can't hear me. But I need to pretend tonight."

She felt her eyes watering and tried to suppress them as best she could before beginning again.

"I know you can't hear me, but I met his family tonight. They live a few blocks from here. Their house is… It's everything ours wasn't. Big, polished, proper. Even their napkins were stiff."

She gave a short, dry laugh.

"You'd have said their dining room looked like a church. Sometimes it got so quiet in there that you could hear a fork scrape. I think his father was trying to be nice, but it wasn't the same niceness you always had. It felt measured somehow – measured in its distribution. It wasn't quite the same as kindness."

Alvina shifted, turning her head toward the window.

"His mother didn't look at me much and said hardly anything to me at all. She floated around like a ghost, serving everything, clearing everything, not sitting still for more than a minute. Is that what I'm supposed to become?"

She was quiet for a while. The city outside murmured faintly, carriages on side streets, a dog barking, someone laughing a block away. For a moment, she felt silly talking into the darkness and told herself to stop it and go to bed. But the desire to speak proved too much.

"Lawrence kissed me on the porch. It was… sweet. He said he's falling in love with me. Or that he loves me – I can't remember. It happened so fast. And I might love him, too. I do. But Mama, I don't know -"

And her whisper trailed off, as she realized she didn't know what it was she didn't know. A strong feeling was resonating within her, that much she knew. But though she felt there must have been an answer to the feeling, a way to resolve it, Alvina felt too lost to understand what the corresponding question was that she needed to ask herself. It was as though she'd been given a test written in a foreign language. More than any other time in her life, Alvina felt the full weight of the impediment of her abnormal childhood. Her thoughts shifted.

"I didn't tell him about the tunnel, or about the rags we stuffed under the door to keep out the wind. I know I didn't need to tell him tonight, but I don't know if I can ever tell him about any of it. Ever."

She took a deep breath and closed her eyes.

"You always said a good man doesn't care about where you've come from, only who you are. But what if his family does? What if I spend my life sitting quietly at someone else's table? And what if he becomes like his father as we get older – what do I do then? I wish you were here to tell me if this is what love is supposed to feel like."

Alvina thought of a novel she'd read a while ago, where the protagonist could feel the hand of a deceased relative gently passing over their cheek the night after they passed. She thought of what her mother's hand had felt like on her cheek and tried hard to believe whatever it is one must consider, to let fantasy slip into reality. But she could not remember the physical sensation she sought out, and soon realized the only feelings left to her were those of exhaustion and loneliness.

Chapter 7

The amount of free time Alvina had in her hands once Lawrence left quickly began to eat away at her. Nights she had once spent out dancing or seeing a movie with Lawrence were now spent either with her friends or, more often, alone in her bedroom. So, it was three weeks after he'd left for bootcamp that Alvina registered to volunteer for the Red Cross.

Alvina moved through life with quiet determination for the next eighteen months. She worked her shifts at the freight company, then rolled bandages at the Red Cross during the evenings. Often, she'd come home well after her friends had eaten dinner, and so she ate alone in silence. Her girlfriends tried their best to include her, pulling her to newsreels at the local theater, inviting her on walks to the market. Still, it was never the same without Lawrence, and she often cited the fatigue her volunteering work caused her as a means of avoiding doing anything too tiring.

Still, each night before bed, no matter how tired she was, Alvina lit the small lamp by her desk and sat with her pen and paper. She wrote to him every single night. Sometimes, she would write a whole letter in one night. Other nights she wrote as little as a sentence or two, and a few nights she ended up erasing more than she wrote.

Lawrence wrote back as often as he could, though never daily. Alvina noticed how his handwriting had grown tighter, more slanted.

He spoke little of what his new life was like, asking more often about how Alvina and her friends were getting on, or whether she had seen his family since he'd left. If the war was as bad as some of the girls at the freight company made it out to seem, Lawrence told her very little of such horrors. The most common thing he wrote about was the mud. It was everywhere, he'd say, and it got in everything.

She didn't hear from his parents at all, though Lawrence suggested she might. Whether they chose to keep their distance or didn't know what to say, Alvina couldn't be sure. She didn't press. Lawrence's letters were enough.

Time passed as such. Shortly after Lawrence left, rationing increased dramatically. Ingredients like sugar, flour, butter, and meat were exceptionally scarce. Alvina's boarding house began serving stew or soup nearly every day, while restaurants raised prices or closed early.

Church dances were cancelled right after Lawrence left. Sometimes Alvina would joke with herself that like herself, America hadn't taken the war seriously until Lawrence went.

With so little worth buying available during this time, Alvina saved most of her money. One night when she especially missed Lawrence, she found a small wooden box at the back of her closet and pinned the only photo of the two she had to its side. On the back of the picture, she wrote 'For our future.' From then on, not a day went by that Alvina didn't slip a few dollars into the box, if not more. The larger the sum became, the more clearly, she could see what it would buy the couple; a white cottage, a vegetable garden, and a small yard with marigolds in the summer. A body of water in the distance, the sea or a lake, she couldn't tell. A husband who loved her. Maybe a baby or two, and a dog to chase them.

On November 11, 1918, the armistice was declared. Alvina would never forget how church bells rang across the city that day, and people poured into the streets with an infectious energy of ecstasy and near delirium. Factory whistles blew. Strangers hugged each other on the sidewalks. The war was over.

Alvina felt as though she had been awakened from a dream when she first heard the news on the street. She did some mental math she'd long put off recognizing and realized that the duration in which she'd been sending letters back and forth with Lawrence was four times as long as their in-person relationship had lasted. The thought staggered her a little. The letter that came a week later staggered her even more.

"We survived trench warfare and a cold winter, so we can wait a little longer to come home. It's not the waiting I mind, it's the longing."

Repatriation was not to be the instant return as so many had expected. Lawrence told her it might take months, and Alvina began to worry as to how many months, as 1919 came along. The waiting stretched into spring, at which time a slow trickle of men started to come in at last. Many celebrated the return of the soldiers; a few noted how much older they looked; how markedly different their demeanors had become from a couple of years ago. A couple of girls at the freight company bragged about all their husbands accomplished. Others grew more excited, believing their husbands and lovers must be almost home by now. But Alvina only grew nervous, for Lawrence's stream of letters abruptly ended in February.

Then one morning in May 1919, a letter arrived at the boardinghouse. It had an odd fold at the bottom and was a little heavier than the others she'd received. The next day, a telegram arrived.

Arriving Indianapolis station Friday. Noon train. L.

The train station in Indianapolis was teeming with people that Friday. Mothers clutched small children. Elderly fathers craned their necks. Sweethearts stood on tiptoe, watching every uniformed man who stepped off.

Alvina met Lawrence's parents at the station, though little was said between them. This was largely due to their shared nerves about Lawrence's return, which hindered their ability and desire to engage in small talk. Alvina noticed that Lawrence's sister was not with them but felt it best not to bring up the fact.

They walked to the platform together and waited there for a good while, the train being delayed at some earlier stop. Alvina wore the small velvet hat with a ribbon she'd worn on their first official date, and which Lawrence had complimented so enthusiastically. Her hands rubbed one another nervously.

The train was a full half hour late when it finally came, and it hissed so loudly as it rolled to a stop that babies cried and younger children covered their ears. Alvina hardly noticed any of this; she'd grown faint the moment she saw its shape forming in the distance.

And then he was there. His duffel was slung over one shoulder as he walked out. He spotted his parents first, and before Alvina could say a word, Lawrence's mother had thrown her arms around him. He embraced her, then approached his father, who hugged him rather stiffly, Alvina felt.

Then Lawrence turned in the opposite direction and began scanning the rest of the platform. The place was as busy as Alvina had ever seen it, full of rushing people, loud embraces, and angry passengers themselves trying to go against the current and get on the train. Alvina soon realized Lawrence had not seen her yet. He did a full revolution, craning his neck this way and that. At last, he turned back towards his parents, and as he was about to ask them something, he caught her eye.

Alvina stood frozen; her breath caught in her chest. He dropped his duffel and embraced her instantaneously. She let her face be buried against his coat, which smelt faintly of wool and earth. She tried to say something and, again, found she could not.

A cry from Lawrence's mother broke the two up. The couple began to weave against the crowd with outstretched hands. When the four of them were finally reunited, Lawrence's father laughed heartily and said it was about time they got home – everyone was waiting for them there. Lawrence suggested he and Alvina might get something to eat together first, as he was so hungry and they hadn't seen each other in so long.

"Well, we've been waiting as long, haven't we?" Lawrence's mother said. "And there's so much food at home already – I made enough to feed twenty of us!"

So it was that the couple did not get a moment alone until they arrived at Lawrence's house, at which point he was finally able to coax a minute's reprieve from his parents before going inside.

"I didn't know if you were alive," Alvina said.

"We couldn't send letters while we were traveling," Lawrence said. "But I sent one a week ago, when we got back to America. Did you get it yet? It's important – it has something quite expensive in it, and I was worried it might get stolen in the mail since I didn't hide it very well. I should've waited until I got here - but I couldn't - but now I'm worried it might not have gotten here at all –"

Seeing he might go on indefinitely if she didn't stop him, Alvina grabbed his right hand with her left.

"Look," was all she said. He looked. The ring he'd sent her in the letter now rested on her finger.

"So, you mean that –"

She nodded and gave a teary smile.

"We've already waited long enough."

Lawrence laughed, choked, and was raw. "Then let's not waste any more time."

He took her hand. They kissed, then walked inside. Alvina thought of the letter she had almost mailed to Lawrence. She'd planned on sending it out that afternoon, before the telegram came in. It had been the easiest letter to write by far.

Yes. A thousand times, yes.

Then they were inside, and Lawrence made the big announcement.

Chapter 8

In the hopeful shadow of the Great War's end, Alvina, Lawrence, and the rest of the world braced for peace but were instead met by another kind of devastation. Invisible, relentless, and without reason, the Spanish flu wreaked even greater havoc on the couple's lives.

Two of Alvina's older stepsiblings died at the height of the outbreak. Her father, already worn thin by sorrow and illness, followed the next Christmas. The grief was heavy and quiet, with no funerals being held and transportation options severely limited, all Alvina could do was pray for the dead. Lawrence lost both of his maternal grandparents, who had passed while he was still in France. But he gave himself so little time to grieve, believing it his duty, as husband and as a man, to be there for the more affected Alvina.

One evening, not long before their wedding, Alvina stood by the narrow window in the small room of Lawrence's apartment. They were taking a break, tired from moving Alvina's heavier items into Lawrence's tiny apartment.

A great fog had descended on the city, so that she could hardly see across the street. She watched as a few masked pedestrians passed by, shoulders hunched against the wind.

"I feel like you came home to a different world," she said. Lawrence turned to her. He, too, had been staring out the window from his chair, though not at any one thing.

"It looks the same to me, if only a bit different here and there."

He said it as reassuringly as he could, but Alvina caught the break in his voice. Indeed, before Alvina had begun talking, Lawrence had been on a similar strain of thought. He had been thinking of how the world as it was now reminded him of a puzzle. Only he hadn't seen the cracks of the pieces before he left, hadn't appreciated the fluidity with which they came perfectly together. Now he could see the cracks. Now it was as though someone had rearranged all the pieces beyond his power for correction, and at times he'd even noticed how holes had formed in the puzzle, as though someone had removed a piece here or there when he'd turned his head the other way. Then he'd try to remember what the piece was, but found he could not, and would get angry, upset, and tired with how everything had changed so much. But he couldn't tell Alvina these things; she needed him now, and he had to be there for her.

"No, it's different," Alvina continued. "And I think it feels like a new world to everyone, too."

Lawrence dismissed the idea and came to hold Alvina, but she remained rigid and brooding as he did so. Soon, he excused himself to go outside for a cigarette. It was one of the habits he'd taken up during the war.

Their wedding day, like so many in those strange months, was quiet and quick. It reminded Alvina of her mother's second wedding in many ways.

Churches were still closed to gatherings at the time, and most ministers were either tending to the sick or ill like them. So, on a clear Wednesday morning in early November, they were married by a Justice of the Peace on the courthouse steps. He spoke behind a mask, and Alvina had hardly heard him when he asked if she'd take Lawrence to be her husband. It was only when she heard him say 'in sickness or in health,' that she realized her part was coming up.

Lawrence's best friend from high school, Samuel, and Alvina's two roommates were the only ones who showed up.

Lawrence had pulled Alvina close and kissed her firmly, boldly, peeling away her mask as he did so. It was a kiss for *now*, not *someday*.

She laughed in his chest. "That's the most reckless thing I've seen anyone do in months."

He smiled at her in such a way that she could never forget.

They had crossed the street afterward to a quiet corner café, one of the few still open for takeout. The windows were fogged. The booths were spaced far apart. The scent of roasted coffee and cinnamon had lingered faintly in the air.

They sat at a small table by the window, sipping hot drinks from mismatched mugs. The waitress brought them a small plate of warm pastries, no charge.

"This wasn't how I imagined my wedding day," Alvina said, looking out at the quiet street. "But it's perfect. Just us."

Lawrence reached across the table, brushing his fingers against hers. "I'll make it up to you someday.

Maybe we'll have a second ceremony. A bigger, better wedding."

And he began to describe it in detail, with that same radiating smile on his face emerging once more.

Lawrence had been given back his old job with the transit company, and Alvina continued working her shifts at the freight company. Their days were long, practical, and mostly unremarkable, but there was a steadiness with it that Alvina found comfort in waking early, eating breakfast downstairs, going to the kitchen to pack each of their small lunch bags, and leaving to catch the same bus, and being with Lawrence through it all.

Alvina finished moving into Lawrence's apartment the weekend after the wedding. A typical bachelor pad, the room had felt cramped enough on those few instances Alvina had been inside it before he'd left. Now it felt twice as small, what with two people and their few possessions tucked into every available corner. A wooden crate served as their nightstand, and Lawrence kept his folded work uniforms stacked neatly in a trunk at the foot of the bed.

Lawrence's idiosyncrasies soon became a part of Alvina's routine as well. He would leave his socks draped on the chair, his papers scattered on the nightstand, and his coat shrugged off onto the bed without a second thought. Usually, she'd try to gently remind him how these things made her feel, how she needed to have a clean space to live in, and usually, he'd correct it. But she did her best to appreciate things as they came. Even this limited domestic life, one room, rationed meals, whispered evenings felt like something sacred: the beginning of their life, however humble—a life they would build together.

Then one evening in late January, Lawrence slid a folded newspaper clipping across the dining room table.

"What's this?" Alvina asked.

"Read it."

She unfolded the clipping and read slowly. It was short, a few paragraphs, but her brow furrowed deeper with each line.

"Land out west," Lawrence said as she read. "Homesteading. Wyoming."

"What about it?" was all Alvina dared to say.

"I was thinking about talking to my dad about it. The paper says that all we have to do is live on some land out there for five years, and then it's ours legally. What do you think of that?" Lawrence said eagerly. "We would have to improve the land, it says, but I imagine that shouldn't be too hard. Nothing more than building a home on it anyway."

"But Wyoming? That's so far from here, isn't it?"

"Over a thousand miles," he said, "But what else is there for us here?"

The sincerity in Lawrence's voice rattled Alvina.

"Your family. Our jobs."

"Alvina, we can't stay here forever. Even if we save up, our jobs don't pay well enough for us to ever move into the type of house I know we deserve."

She thought of her drawer of cash, the one with their only picture tagged to it. There were hundreds of dollars in it now. The thought that it wouldn't be enough for them to make it here rattled her even further, more because she suspected Lawrence was right in his claim.

"But we have each other here," she countered, trying to hide the hurt from her voice. "I know it's been a while, but I still feel like I got you back from the war yesterday. If we do this –"

"We'd still be together there," Lawrence interrupted. "If anything, even more so than here. It'd be just us out there, once we get settled. We'll have so much more room to breathe out there. Do you want to live like this our whole lives, Alvina?" He gestured to their cramped surroundings. "I know we deserve more than this. I know *you* deserve more."

"I've never been more than fifty miles from here," Alvina said calmly as she set the clipping down carefully.

"I hadn't either, until the war. But now I want something new. Something bigger than this. Something we can build from the ground up."

Alvina looked at Lawrence as firmly as she could.

"I don't want to go."

"But Alvina –"

"No, Lawrence." It was her turn to interrupt him. "I want to stay here awhile longer, at the very least. I can't move a thousand miles away from here – my job, my friends – because you want something new. I can't believe you can even consider our doing something like this, after all we've done to get so far here."

He eyed her coldly, taking the newspaper clipping back before leaving the room. They didn't talk about the matter again that night. They didn't talk about anything after that. It proved to be the first time in their marriage that they had gone to bed without resolving the issues of the day.

Alvina felt as though resentment was radiating from Lawrence when he turned away from her and curled himself up tightly as soon as they got into bed. She wanted to say something, not to let whatever air had settled upon them now ferment into something even worse. But she could not find it in herself to speak, and Lawrence said nothing.

It was a cold evening in late February when Lawrence brought up the land again. They had finished supper, cabbage stew, and two thick slices of dry cornbread. Alvina was washing dishes in the kitchen. Lawrence remained in the dining room, reading the newspaper.

When Alvina returned from the kitchen, Lawrence casually laid the paper out on the table. He did not push it her way, but he made sure it was open enough and flat enough that Alvina could read the headline from afar.

"A family in Illinois moved out west. They said they got six hundred acres, since there were so many of them. Imagine having six hundred acres all to yourself. I don't know what I'd do with it."

"You're still thinking about this," she said.

He nodded.

"Can you blame me? When I'm at work now, and they're having me do things I could do in my sleep, my mind wanders. You know this. Well, what about so much of it being mentioned in the newspapers and by the other guys at work? I can't help but think about what it would be like out there for us. A house we built with our own hands. Land no one can take away from us. No rent. No landlords. No cramped bedroom and tripping over each other on our way out the door, either."

Lawrence began to smile unconsciously as he talked, a smile that widened as he went. Alvina was reminded of the smile from their wedding day. At the sight of this smile, Alvina herself began to smile as well, but she quickly caught herself and pursed her lips.

"But Wyoming?" she said. "You say you talk to the men at work about it. Well, I've talked to the girls at my work about it too, since you brought it up. They say it's nothing but prairie out there. Empty. Cold. No police to keep you from getting robbed and killed, either."

Lawrence leaned forward, elbows on his knees.

"They don't know what they're talking about. But don't you want that? Something no one has handed us. Something we build for ourselves?"

"No one's ever handed me anything," she said, retiring to the bedroom to put an end to the conversation. There she began to fold laundry on the bed.

A plain wooden cabin, wind howling at the door. A garden that took years to tame. A well dug too shallow, then too deep. Blisters. Dirt under her nails. No shops. No dresses in the windows. No neighbors to borrow sugar from. No help. That's what would be out there for them if they made it there at all. She was sure of it. Not the white cottage of her dreams, nor the vegetable garden or marigolds. They have no ocean to look out on, and no safe place for their kids to grow up and go to school. She was sure of that, too.

Alvina looked across the room. Again, Lawrence's socks were draped over his chair. She sighed as she went to gather them.

She wondered whether this was what Mrs. Hursting did for her husband. An image of the pale, dutiful woman came to Alvina. Bustling about, always busy and always spoken for.

"Lawrence!" she yelled, calling him in from the other room. She'd had enough. Of the sock nonsense. Of Homestead nonsense. Both would be set straight, once and for all.

But then Lawrence came in and rushed to the chair before she could say anything.

"Oh, I'm sorry, Alvina, I didn't mean to forget. I'm trying to be better, really am. Here," he said, scooping up the rest of the laundry from the bed. "Let me take this for you. I'll fold it tonight, out in the kitchen. You've done enough already. Then you'll know how sorry I am, too."

And before she could say anything, he was out of the room. Alvina, a bit dazed by the rapidity of it all, lay down on the bed.

He can be sweet when he sees how much I need it.

She did need it, too, because she was thoroughly exhausted. Cooking for two, cleaning for two. Moving all her things over to Lawrence's apartment, then organizing them once they were there. Not to mention her job. Even sleeping in bed with Lawrence was tough for her. Sometimes she'd wake up in the night and almost scream, so accustomed to being alone. It kept her from sleeping well, so that now, as she watched Lawrence poorly fold the laundry through the ajar bedroom door, she couldn't help but let her head rest against the cool pillow. She told herself she'd only rest her head a minute, since there was still so much to do before going to bed. Then she'd help Lawrence do the laundry right, then tell him, firmly but kindly, that they were never, never going to Wyoming. She played over her plan of attack in her head behind shut eyelids, then fell asleep almost instantaneously.

Chapter 9

The idea of moving to Wyoming stayed in Lawrence's mind a great deal in the following months. Alvina, too busy with work, chores, and trying to make Lawrence's apartment a space worth living in, could not find the strength in herself to kill Lawrence's dream once and for all. She had slowly noticed him growing increasingly distant from her after she'd moved in, and the thought of furthering this divide was too much for her to deal with at the time. Besides, he was so happy when he talked of the frontier.

"What harm is there in letting him dream of such things?" she'd tell herself on certain nights. But she knew, sooner or later, she'd have to shut down the idea for good.

For his part, Lawrence committed himself to playing the long game. He knew Alvina was cautious by nature and that the unknowns of frontier life unsettled her. However, by working at it little by little, he hoped to change her mind slowly. During their dinners, he'd consciously drop small details of this or that story he'd heard of successes out west. He also began to complain about how small their apartment was and how he'd like to have a much bigger house someday. Occasionally, he'd even play into Alvina's desires for kids, pointing out all the pitfalls their apartment had as an environment to raise a baby in. But much to Lawrence's chagrin, Alvina appeared little warmer to the idea months later than when he'd first brought it up. Imagining it would take years before she'd even consider the idea, Lawrence eventually realized that, for change to come, either a grand gesture would need to be made, or a bargain struck.

So it was that one evening, after yet another circular conversation, Lawrence exhaled heavily and tossed what Alvina believed to be yet another folded newspaper article onto the table. But when she opened it, she did not see the article about the West she had expected.

"You *resigned*?"

Lawrence didn't meet her searching eyes but instead looked out the window as he spoke.

"I can't work there forever."

It was the coldest she'd ever heard his voice.

"But we can barely afford to live here as it is!"

It was true. Rent prices had been significantly raised once Lawrence came back, and neither of the two seemed to be able to be promoted anytime soon. Especially now.

"We'll figure something out," he said.

"This is about going west again. Lawrence, we can't do that. You know we can't. *I* can't do that."

To Alvina's surprise, Lawrence didn't push the matter. He got up from the table, excused himself from dinner, and then retired to the bedroom.

Alvina only noticed something was wrong when she got back from work the next day and saw Lawrence still hadn't left the bed.

"Maybe he needs a day off before he starts looking for a new job," she thought to herself.

But Lawrence wouldn't get out of bed for the next few days, either. Alvina was forced to bring his meals into the bedroom as if he were sick. And in many ways, he looked the part. His face took on the pale tone of the dying, and he said nothing to Alvina even when she pressed him. As far as appearances went, there was only one significant difference between a sick man and Lawrence's present condition. Alvina noted it constantly. Tucked in bed as he was, his countenance did not resemble that of an ailing man. Just the opposite; every time Alvina saw him, she could tell he was deep in thought. Thinking, always thinking. Thinking what, she knew not, and it scared her increasingly as the days passed.

At first, she brought the frontier up only to get a reaction out of Lawrence. It didn't work. No matter what she said, he remained unflinching, his eyes fixed on the walls in a dull stare. But soon it was all Alvina could think of doing to coax him out of his near-comatose state.

She began asking about what water sources would be out there. What would the planting seasons be like? How far would they have to go to reach the nearest doctor? At times, Alvina thought she could sense him cracking, eager to give her an answer. But now it was his turn to remain stoic with her; he said nothing to her, no matter what she asked.

Without even knowing it, Alvina began making packing lists in the margins of her prayer journal. She began to count the dollars saved in her small chest and calculate how far it would get them. She began to fall asleep at work. Late into the night, she would start legitimately considering whether they could make it to Wyoming in their current state. They'd have to go soon, too, or else they'd begin to eat into Alvina's savings too much.

After a week had passed and Lawrence had yet to get out of bed, Alvina called Lawrence's family for help. She hated the idea of leaning on them for support so early into their marriage, but she had hit the wall by then.

They came over one Saturday afternoon, a bit confused by Alvina's request. After three hours of talking to an unfazed Lawrence, Alvina saw they had only made the matter worse.

As his parents left, Lawrence's father pointed out the small drawer of cash, which now sat by the front door. Taped on it with masking tape was the label "Wyoming".

"Don't you start considering going there," Mr. Hursting said rather roughly. "Lawrence will come around in time. This kind of stuff happens to a lot of men his age – they come back from the war and want the same kind of excitement they had over there. But he'll come around, don't you worry."

Ironically, it was at this moment that Alvina's beliefs were at last solidified. She looked at the past that she and Lawrence had laid out for themselves, and the future they might still realize together. And then she knew it was either to be Wyoming with Lawrence, or Indianapolis without him. And she'd have to pick it soon.

She continued to make lists throughout that week about what they would bring, what they would leave behind, what they would have to sell.

One afternoon, Alvina sat cross-legged on the bedroom floor, folding linens and old dish towels. She picked the pile up and began walking towards the drawer to put them away. Only she stopped herself from doing so and instead looked at Lawrence. His gaze met hers, but she felt he was looking through her rather than at her. She made a significant gesture of putting the laundry on the lone chair that stood in the corner of their bedroom.

"We'll have to start packing soon, for Wyoming. These will be the first things we pack."

She thought she saw his eyes flicker a bit, but he said nothing and remained still as ever.

The next day, Alvina bought a large chest from a nearby pawn shop. It was big enough that the manager had to help her carry it to the apartment. They set down the chest in the living room, and as soon as the manager left, Alvina went to the bedroom and told Lawrence what she'd done. Again, she thought she saw his eyes flicker, so she was moved to begin clearing the dinner table immediately and then opened the chest. She had packed half of the kitchen's belongings into the chest that night. Then, as she made her way into bed, she began to cry. When she tried to stop, her tears only came more, and her choking only grew louder.

"I can't do this alone," she said. "I can't, I can't."

The next morning, Alvina heard a rustling in the kitchen. It scared her so much she didn't even notice Lawrence's side of the bed was empty, and she seemed more surprised to see her husband at work in the kitchen than if she'd seen a stray animal or a burglar instead.

"I'm thinking we wrap the dishes in the dish cloths, so that they don't break," he said. Then, to show her what he meant, he stacked five of the dishes together before folding a dishrag over their tops and sides. It was as though the last week was nothing more than a bad dream. But something *had* changed during those seven days, something she'd have to live with forever now.

"So," she thought to herself as she watched him fold more dishrags around dishes, "Wyoming it is."

After they finished packing all but the barest of essentials, Alvina asked Lawrence what their next step was. He led her to the bedroom, where he dropped down on his stomach and reached beneath the bed. From there, he pulled out a thick manila folder she'd never seen before.

Back at the dining room table, he spread out the papers it contained. It was everything a person needed to move West, and then some. Lawrence at once began filling out those few forms he hadn't already completed; in her turn, Alvina began to read whatever form was available, trying to soak in as much of the information as possible.

When they sealed the last envelope and licked the stamp, Lawrence handed it to Alvina. "You should mail it," he said. "Your office is close to the post office."

She nodded and thought of how she'd have to quit her job in a few weeks now, if not sooner. Yet more than a few weeks passed before a thick envelope finally arrived—stamped from the State of Wyoming, Office of Homestead Claims.

Lawrence flushed with excitement at the sight of the envelope while Alvina let out a mental sigh of relief. They had eaten into her savings a good deal during those several weeks, both to feed themselves and to prepare for the trip. She didn't know how much longer they could've survived at their current pace.

"Read it aloud," Alvina said as Lawrence opened the envelope. A look of consternation came over Lawrence, as he wanted to scan every page immediately. But he bit his tongue and nodded.

He read the first page aloud, stumbling over some of the words in excitement. It said little that the couple didn't already know.

"How will we find our land?" Alvina asked once he finished reading the first page.

Lawrence shuffled through the pages. He stopped at the end.

"According to the paperwork, we report to the land office in Cheyenne," Lawrence said. "They'll give us the coordinates—section, township, and range."

"Coordinates? Not an address?"

Lawrence couldn't help cracking a grin.

"Nope. But we'll be alright. All we must do is follow the instructions. We'll probably have to get there by horse and wagon. Don't worry too much, though. I've got a compass packed."

Alvina's brow furrowed.

"What if there aren't any markers to show us the way?"

"Then we ask someone to direct us. A rancher, a deputy, a mail carrier—someone will know."

Some of Alvina's anxieties from before began to resurface. But she only nodded her head slowly, folding her hands in her lap. "I … I want to be sure we can do this."

Lawrence took one of her hands in his.

"We'll make it fine. I promise."

He began reading the rest of the papers.

They spent the following days carefully packing their three trunks. Weight restrictions limited what they could bring—if any of the trunks were too heavy at the station, they'd either be forced to leave the things behind or pay a fee they could no longer afford. The letter advised them to bring three trunks in total, the maximum allowed—one per traveler and a third for tools and provisions for the whole party.

In the tool and provisions trunk, they packed a hammer, a saw, an axe, a small anvil, and a rifle Lawrence inherited from his grandfather, nestled between two boxes of ammunition.

Alvina's trunk, the one she'd bought from the pawn shop, ended up being a kitchen-in-a-box. In it were two cast-iron pans, her enamelware dishes wrapped in tea towels, spoons and knives, and the heavy tin coffee pot Lawrence insisted on bringing.

Lawrence's trunk served as their survival kit. A roll of bandages, a tin of salve, handmade soap wrapped in wax paper, bags of dried beans, dried canned peaches and raisins, sacks of flour, and one oil lantern with its fragile globe swaddled in Alvina's wool shawl. Around each item, they wrapped clothing—underwear, wool socks, shirts, coats, sweaters, and boots.

The last couple of days were spent taking care of those remaining loose ends. Alvina officially quit her job the day after receiving the letter from Wyoming. They closed their bank accounts the next day. Lawrence counted the contents of his savings jar three times before placing the bills into oilcloth bags, each tied tightly and hidden in the bottoms of the trunks. Alvina carried a wad of bills in a secret pocket hidden in the side seam of her dress. The Wyoming drawer remained tucked away at the bottom of her trunk, though it had only half as much cash in it now as on the day Lawrence quit his job.

On their final Sunday in Indianapolis, they walked together to Mass. At the same church where they'd first danced under the flickering lights of the parish hall, Alvina remembered how they had sat together in the corner the first time they'd met. Then she remembered all the dances that came in the following weeks, in that blissful period before the war. Would she and Lawrence ever dance like that again, out in Wyoming?

After Mass, the parishioners surprised them with a modest going-away gathering in the church community room. The priest offered a special blessing for their journey, sprinkling holy water on their heads and clasping their hands as he prayed for their safe passage.

"You are brave souls," he said warmly. "But you are not alone."

Lawrence's family saw them off at the train station the day of their departure. Alvina sensed quiet resentment in both Lawrence's parents, so that she began to suspect they blamed her for what was happening. But what did it matter? They might never see Lawrence again after today. She had won his influence in this sense, but what a hollow victory it was.

"To think, it was less than a year ago when you came back to us here. And now you're going again," Lawrence's father said as they arrived at the station.

Mrs. Hursting began crying once they made it to the platform. His father had to wrestle her off her son once the train came into view. He then gave the two a solemn nod and led his wife down the station stairs. Alvina felt a little guilty that she was so relieved to see them go.

"I'll write as soon as I find a post office," Lawrence called out to them, his voice thick with emotion.

The two loaded Alvina's big trunk first, once the train was ready for boarding. They then came back for Lawrence's and the tool trunk. To the mild astonishment of both, the station's steel scale declared each of the three trunks was comfortably below the weight necessary to avoid any overage fees.

As a parting gift, Lawrence's parents had purchased a private room on the train for the couple. As Alvina shut the door of this room behind her, she turned to see Lawrence waiting for her on one knee.

"Alvina, I want our marriage to begin now." His voice was a little raspy, from emotion or the early morning, she couldn't tell. After all, they had woken up at five to catch this train. "I'm sorry for how I was then," he continued, "before we decided to go. But I think I can be a husband worthy of you now. Someone who will love you and be there with you through it all." He began to tear up. "It just – I'm just so happy I've found someone like you, who's willing to put up with me through all this. To go to the end of the earth to make me happy."

Alvina teared up as well.

"You know I'll always love you, Lawrence. You don't have to do all this."

"But I want to!" He said, jumping up from his one knee to stand closer to her. "I want to do all this and more for you. I want to give you that big wedding I promised and that big house I've been talking about so much."

She took his hand into her own and squeezed it.

"I want all those things too," she said softly, "but there's one thing I want now."

"What is it? Anything at all, tell me and it'll be done."

She gestured to the only bench in the cabin.

"I want to sit here beside you and close my eyes a little while. Can we do that?"

Lawrence grinned.

"Consider it done."

He helped her navigate around the trunks towards the bench, then sat down beside her. She leaned up against him and wrapped her arm under his as they watched through the cabin window, the station slowly moved away.

Chapter 10

They spent the night on the train, lulled to sleep by the rhythmic clatter of the wheels and the hiss of steam. Alvina dozed lightly, resting her head against Lawrence's shoulder, with his arm wrapped protectively around her. Lawrence stayed wide awake, watching each small town come and go from their window. He was far too excited to even think of sleep that night.

The sky was beginning to lighten as the train pulled into the Union Station in Denver, with the gray and blue of dawn beginning to replace the dark of night. Still groggy from the journey, they found a modest boardinghouse two blocks from the station. There, they rented a small room for the night, where the bed creaked, the wallpaper was faded, and the wash basin in the corner leaked.

By 7:30 the next morning, they purchased hot coffee and buttered rolls from a vendor cart a block from the boardinghouse. As instructed, they had checked their trunks at the station for safekeeping and boarded the Union Pacific Railroad bound for Cheyenne.

"This land is so flat you can see tomorrow coming," Lawrence said as their train began to leave the station. "The conductor told me one hundred more miles to go. Hopefully, we'll get some mountains soon. I was looking for them all night."

"You slept for a few hours, though, right?"

Lawrence's only response was to chuckle faintly as he stirred sugar into his coffee.

"Well, it's nothing like Indiana," Alvina said as she turned towards the window. "The sky looks much bigger out here."

Over the next couple of hours, Alvina spent much of the trip watching this sky shrink and grow. It grew to its largest as they pulled into the Cheyenne train station.

They arrived minutes before noon. Seeing the indecision on their faces, one of the station's railroad agents quickly approached the couple after they got off the train.

"Settlers, I imagine?" he said somewhat genially, and soon he and Lawrence began talking of the trip he and Alvina were now on and where they needed to go next. Lawrence spoke with gaiety that almost astounded Alvina, who, for her part, felt flustered by the agent. Where Lawrence saw an opportunity to speak of the grand adventure the couple was embarking on, Alvina felt unsettled by having been so easily marked as newcomers. Was it so obvious they didn't belong in a place like this?

But her fears only had a moment to linger. In a second, the agent pointed the couple toward the State Capitol building, a few blocks away, then moved on to assist another idle pair. Lawrence double-checked that their trunks were securely locked, then hoisted the three trunks onto a rented dolly and headed in the instructed direction without saying a word. Flustered, Alvina grabbed the rest of their belongings and tried to catch up with Lawrence as best she could.

Alvina was struck by the bustle of the street as soon as she stepped outside—wagons, carriages, and families streaming in and out. It rattled her enough that she had to stop a moment and gather herself, even as Lawrence pressed on further without her. Finally, with a last deep breath, Alvina steeled herself as best she could and began to run after Lawrence. It was awkward and tiring to run carrying several bags and bundles, and Alvina only caught up to Lawrence as he was approaching the steps of the grand sandstone Capitol building.

"Lawrence!" she cried out as he began up the first step. But he didn't hear her, and she had to cry out twice before he turned around and saw his wife, now hunched over and drenched in sweat.

"Geez, Al!" he said, descending the stairs to prop her up. "You alright? Walking a few blocks shouldn't make you *this* tired."

"That's because I ran," she said through heavy breaths. "You left me behind at the station."

Lawrence recoiled a little.

"Did I? I didn't think I did. I swore you were right behind me the whole time. But then, if I did do that, why didn't you yell after me?"

"You were too far away. You wouldn't have heard me even if I did yell. You barely heard me when I yelled just now."

He gave her a brief glance at searching, trying to figure out the best course of action. After a moment's meditation, he went back up the steps. He then returned with the other two trunks, which he placed down at Alvina's feet.

"You stay here, then, and catch your breath. I'll go in and see if I can do this by myself while you rest a while."

The words made Alvina right herself.

"Lawrence, I don't need that long, give me a minute or so –"

But Lawrence shook his head emphatically.

"I can't wait even one minute, Al. Let me take a quick look. I'll be right back."

And before she could say anything else, he disappeared into the propped-open doors of the Capitol building.

Alvina stood beside the three trunks, alone, for the next three hours. Though she wanted to go in after Lawrence, only minutes after he'd left, she felt the impossibility of such a desire. If she did follow him, who would watch the trunks? And how was she to find him if she did go in? From where she now stood, the Capitol building looked to her the most significant government building she'd ever seen.

So, Alvina waited and waited, growing worried, then frustrated, then angry, then worried again. What if something happened in there? For the first time, she thought of the prospect of being left all alone in such a foreign place as this, and the thought scared her enough that she forgot to be anything but relieved when Lawrence finally came back out. She embraced him tightly when he came back down and had to fight to keep herself from tearing up.

"Whoa there," Lawrence said as she grabbed his waist. "Sorry about that, didn't mean to make you wait that long. But I did everything that needed to be done, so why don't we go get some food finally? I'm starved."

In a nearby diner, Lawrence told Alvina all about what happened at their late lunch.

He began by describing the large red sign he had seen upon entering the Capitol building, marked **"Homestead Claims Office →"**. Following the sign, he'd ended up in a large hallway with several lines about it. There, a state employee handed him a card with a number and told him which line to wait in.

"You should've seen how long that line was. When Horace Greeley said, 'Go west, young man,' people certainly listened."

"I would've liked to see it," Alvina said with tangible sarcasm. Lawrence continued undeterred.

The family that he met in line and talked to, whom he'd talked to for nearly an hour as they all inched forward to the counter. Then, once it was his turn in line, he handed their papers over the counter to a "friendly-enough" looking woman.

"She told me every page was perfect. Said you wouldn't imagine how many people didn't bring their paperwork with them, and how many more did it all wrong. I told her that was all you," he said with a smile. Alvina returned the smile as best she could.

After the woman had stamped their packet with several bold "APPROVED" stamps in dark red ink, another state employee led Lawrence into the claims office.

As best as he could, Lawrence tried to describe the small room he went into next, with its tall shelves lined with maps, ledgers, and government documents. Then he described the man he met in there. Short, stout, with thin spectacles and an accent, the likes of which Lawrence had never heard. He sat behind a desk littered with papers and several open ink pots as Lawrence entered, telling him first to sit at his desk, then asking for the bundle of paper Lawrence was clutching.

"So, you got the land?" Alvina asked. It was the first question she had asked as soon as they sat down at the diner, and it had annoyed her greatly when Lawrence insisted on telling the whole story of his venture in order. Again, Lawrence didn't answer her question.

"I'm getting there, hold on."

Lawrence then described how the man, whom he began referring to as 'the clerk,' slowly examined each page in succession, making little noises now and then that Lawrence couldn't discern the slightest idea from. At last, when he was satisfied with the pages, he put them down on the desk, then flipped open a thick book and dipped his pen into one of the ink pots. He asked Lawrence if he understood the terms of the Homestead Act.

"And I wanted to say, 'better than the back of my hand!' Only I worried that he might think me a bit of a show-off if I said that, and by then I'd figured this man would be the one deciding where we get to live, you know. So, I said I understood it generally but would appreciate it if he told me about the finer details."

The clerk told Lawrence numerous details he already knew, and Lawrence nodded politely until the clerk finished by emphasizing that the land needed to be lived on continuously for five years and that Lawrence and his party must build a dwelling of some kind there.

"Don't know how else you'd live somewhere continuously for five years, but I kept nodding and saying 'yes, sir' all the same. Imagine he has to say that type of stuff for legal purposes and whatnot."

After his speech, the clerk turned the ledger to face Lawrence and tapped a dotted grid on a map of southeastern Wyoming.

"In the end, after everything had been worked out, he gave me this."

Lawrence slid forward the first of the new papers he'd been holding in his right hand. Alvina read the document. Other than a few paragraphs of legal jargon, the only noteworthy lines were those at the bottom, which read:

This is your temporary certificate with the legal description of the property:

26 N 75 W 25 W2 320.00, W2E2 160.00 E2SE 80.00 TOTAL AC: 560.00

DO NOT LOSE.

"Clerk told me the official deed will be processed once residency and improvements are verified. Then he gave me a survey map and instructions on how to travel there."

He held up another of the new papers, one that looked like a map to Alvina.

"The train to Laramie departs twice weekly. Otherwise, the only way to get there is to travel by covered wagon from Cheyenne."

Alvina picked up the temporary deed and folded it with care. Her hands trembled slightly as she tucked it into her handbag.

"What's the place called?" she asked.

"Doesn't have a name yet, apparently. The clerk told me it's by Mule Creek and Medicine Bow, but what does that mean to us? All that matters is that I got it at a steal."

"A steal?" Alvina was confused. "I thought it was all free. He didn't charge you, did he? Lawrence, we don't have the money to be buying free land."

"No, no, that's not what I meant. You see, in Wyoming the homesteading parcels are larger than in any other state. He told me why, but I forgot. But it's huge, Alvina. Five hundred and sixty acres that is about a square mile of land."

"I thought the largest parcel could be a hundred and sixty acres. I guess that is for other states,"

Alvina said, with more concern and less excitement than Lawrence had been expecting.

"There were a few problems with it, and I guess these made getting rid of the parcel tougher than most. You should've seen the face of the clerk when I said we'd take it. He looked as though he'd pulled a fast one on me – only I was the one pulling one over on him! Imagine it, Alvina. Five hundred and sixty acres. There's no water, but it's nothing we can't handle."

"No water?" Alvina's voice broke. "Lawrence, I told you all I wanted – the only thing I asked for was a lake or even a pond to build the house by. I told you that, repeatedly. It was the only thing I asked for. And now you're saying we won't even have water? What are we supposed to do with all that land and no water?"

Lawrence dismissed the concern with a shrug of the shoulders.

"I can't believe there are five hundred and sixty acres out there and not even one with some water. Can't be."

With this, Lawrence began describing what they could do with all that land, all the projects he now had in mind that no 'regular-sized' parcel would've worked for. But Alvina's mind did not see these projects materialize as Lawrence described them, despite the detail. Instead, she saw her dream of the future one final time. A dog, a family, and a house by the lake. Slowly, to the tune of Lawrence's distant, excited voice, the vision began to fade away, until this future Alvina could so clearly see just a few hours ago seemed nothing more than a hazy mirage in the distance.

Chapter 11

After lunch, Lawrence and Alvina asked around about the best way to get from Cheynne to Medicine Bow or Mule Creek. They found out little more than that no trains ran to either town, or that the only stagecoach that went to Mule Creek had a one-trunk-per-person policy. Eventually, Lawrence came up with an idea.

"You know, the clerk at the office told me something I think might work. He said there was a place around here where we could buy a horse and covered wagon. Well, if we did that, we could take all our trunks, no problem."

"Won't that be expensive?"

"Maybe. But do you think we can get on with leaving behind one of these trunks? Besides we will need a horse and wagon eventually."

"That is a big deal. We need the trunks," she said noncommittally.

So it was that, after a night at the first inn they could find, the couple spent the next morning looking for the place the clerk had mentioned. It took them hours to find it, unfamiliar with the street names and landmarks that were to direct them there. They were drenched in sweat by the time they at last found the place.

The place the clerk had referred them to was primarily used as a depot, which was one of the main reasons they struggled to find it initially. It was only because a man of small stature approached them and asked if George had sent them that they didn't turn around and leave almost immediately.

"Is he the clerk who works at the Capitol building?" Lawrence said, having already forgotten the clerk's name.

"That's him," the small man nodded.

Lawrence nodded, and soon the small man led them to a wagon with two horses, Alvina felt would fit their purposes quite well.

"How much would you want for this?" she asked upon seeing the wagon. The small man only laughed in response.

"Afraid this one isn't for sale, missus. No, I need to take you two out to the barn. We only meet customers here since it's so much easier to find than the barn."

Alvina almost laughed at this comment.

"So, we'll be taking this wagon to get there, then?" Lawrence asked.

The man nodded as he untied one of the horse's reins from its post. Alvina and Lawrence tentatively climbed into the back of the wagon as the short man untied the other's reins; it was the first time either of them in their whole lives had been in a wagon. The man then hopped into the front of the wagon, and in a matter of minutes, they were off.

The ride was bumpy and uneventful. Alvina clutched the sides of the cart while Lawrence kept his eyes on the horizon. The small man drove with little concern for his guests. Alvina felt he was more focused on telling the pair how affordable his selection was rather than on the road ahead of them. Something about the man struck Alvina as wily. The way he spoke and the things he said seemed intended to set them both at ease during the trip, and yet had the opposite impression on Alvina.

"Hope you don't mind if we look at the horses first," the man said as the barn came into sight. "It's easier that way, you know."

"Sure, no problem," Lawrence said.

"Why is it easier that way?" Alvina asked. The man pretended not to hear her.

"I don't know if we shouldn't look somewhere else for wagons," she said to Lawrence in a muffled whisper as they pulled in towards the barn. Lawrence jerked back.

"You said you were afraid that the price of buying our wagon would be too high. Now you're worried about them being too cheap. Alvina, we can't have everything perfect. We're going to have to make compromises, you know."

And before she could say anything, Lawrence hopped out of the stationary wagon. With a small sigh of exasperation, she followed him out.

The small man had taken them to a red barn about a mile outside of town. Its paint was faded, and its roof had numerous holes. The smell of hay, horses, and dust hit both Alvina and Lawrence the moment they stepped into the barn.

"Ever handled a horse before?" the small man asked, raising an eyebrow as he unlatched the first stall.

"Only seen them from the train window," Lawrence said, trying to suppress a cough as he did so. Alvina's eyes watered. The man chuckled.

"That's what I figured. Don't worry, I will walk you through it."

He led out a scrawny, chestnut-colored mare. It was notably smaller than the two horses they'd taken to get there and looked half as well-fed. Alvina almost felt sorry for the thing.

"This here's Rosie. She's three years old. Young but steady. No wildness in her. Good temperament, good lungs. I raised her myself."

The horse wheezed a bit as he led it towards the pair. Alvina took a hesitant step closer.

"She's not nearly as tall as your two horses," Alvina commented.

"She's about fifteen hands," George said. "Not too tall, not too short. Strong enough to pull your wagon, but not so heavy she'll eat you dry."

"But why wouldn't we want horses like yours?" Alvina asked. Again, the man pretended not to hear, instead asking Lawrence what he thought of the horse.

"Pretty," he said.

"I think so too," the small concurred. "And for a good price, too. But let's not worry about that yet. Not every day do you get to meet a horse for the first time. Why don't I teach you how to handle her?"

So it was that the next hour, the small man patiently taught Lawrence how to brush down Rosie and a few other, similarly scrawny horses. He then taught Lawrence how to check their hooves and how to slip the halter over their ears. Alvina tried to follow along but quickly became overwhelmed. She instead sat in the background, watching.

Thinking. At one point, the thought crossed her mind that, if the small man had taken them further out of town, he might have easily robbed or even killed them without anyone noticing or caring. The thought gave her a visceral chill. Thankfully, there were enough houses nearby that she felt such a thing couldn't happen now, but what if it had? They had gotten into the wagon without the slightest thought to such an occurrence, and yet... She tried to dispel the thoughts from her mind as best she could.

After the lesson, they moved over to the wagon yard behind the barn. Three full wagons stood in a row, each with curved arched covers made of heavy canvas. Numerous stray wagon parts littered the ground around them.

"Ever since the Homestead Act was announced, we've been selling wagons faster than we can make them. As of right now, these three are all we got, unfortunately," the small man explained, patting the nearest one.

It was the biggest of the three. "Small is fine for light travel. Medium fits two trunks and gear. But is this big beauty? Ten feet long, four feet wide, and sideboards a good four feet high. She could take you and all your goods to the Pacific, let alone over to Medicine Bow."

Lawrence nodded slowly. "And the wheels?"

"Rear wheels are five feet across, front about three and a half," George said. "Steel rims, oak spokes. My brother makes 'em strong. You'll feel it roll, but she'll last."

Alvina stepped towards the small wagon.

"I think this one could work," she said, eying it over. The small man made a noise of disapproval.

"You said you had three trunks, didn't you? That one can hardly carry one. And trust me, it'll feel even smaller once you're living in it."

"Lawrence, come take a look and let me know what you think."

Lawrence moved from the large wagon to the smallest, cautiously inspecting it.

"I think we could fit at least two trunks in here," he said at last. "Three would probably be pushing it, though."

"What about this one, then?" Alvina asked, referring to the medium-sized wagon.

"You said this one could do two trunks and gear?" Lawrence asked the man, pointing to the medium-sized wagon.

"What about three trunks and no gear?"

The man shook his head.

"Maybe, but I wouldn't try it."

Lawrence turned towards Alvina.

"Well, if he lives out here and he won't try it, I don't know that we ought to."

"But he's not the one who will be buying it, either," Alvina said in a hushed, acidic voice.

"Look, the biggest one is going to be the most expensive one. Of course, he wants us to buy it. I say we either get this one," Alvina pointed to the medium-sized wagon, "or look elsewhere."

"But where else is there to look?" Lawrence said loudly enough that the small man, who had been inspecting the back of one of the wagons, returned to the couple and began describing all the best features of the biggest wagon.

Lawrence kicked at the dusty ground in contemplation as the man went on. By now, the sun was at its highest, and sweat had again drenched the two. In time, Lawrence recognized that, more than anything else right now, he wanted to be done with the deal. Then they could get out of the heat. Then they could finally get on their way to all that land that was so eagerly awaiting them. If the small man thought they should go with the bigger one, who were they to argue?

He looked at Alvina as the man spoke. Her eyes were wide; lips pressed into a tight line. He got the impression that she was impatiently waiting for him to make a choice. This impression wasn't far from the truth, either, so Alvina was relieved when Lawrence interrupted the man to announce they'd made a decision.

"We'll take Rosie and the large wagon," Lawrence said, voice steady. "How much do you want for them?"

"Lawrence!" Alvina shouted. She couldn't help it; she had already let him take away her house on the water the day before by leaving matters in his hands. To let it happen again, this time before her very eyes, was too much.

"Hold on," Lawrence responded, anticipating the outburst, "Let the man tell us the prices first. They might not be as bad as you think? Right?"

Lawrence said, turning a genial smile towards the small man. He, in turn, quoted a price for the horse and the biggest wagon that made both their stomachs twist.

"Two-hundred fifty dollars."

"That's too much, Lawrence," Alvina said. "You know we can't afford that."

"It is a bit much," Lawrence said to the man. "Couldn't you go a little lower?"

The man quoted a sum of five dollars less than his original estimate, then said he wouldn't go any lower than that.

"That's not too bad for what we're getting, isn't it, Alvina?" Lawrence now said to his wife, who in turn merely shook her head.

"Quit it, Lawrence. We can't do that either. You know what you need to say," Alvina said, nodding to the wagon on which the man had taken the couple to the barn. "Now say it and let's be on our way."

Lawrence nodded solemnly, then turned back towards the man.

"You heard the woman," he said to the man as dispassionately as he could muster, who, in response, looked at Lawrence as to say, 'Are you so stupid as to let such a deal slip out of your hands?' A staring contest ensued for the next few seconds, broken at last by Lawrence.

"We can't do anything more than two hundred and thirty-five dollars. You're going to have to take us back into town with nothing if you can't do that."

Alvina thought she saw the smallest of grins creep over the small man for a fraction of a second, but he did well to hide it if so, for he sank into a stern, meditative gaze at Lawrence for a few moments after he'd spoken. At last, he said,

"Well, I won't make anything off of it but seeing as you and your wife have been so nice all day, and that I know you two will need it so much, I guess I can do two thirty-five."

Lawrence nearly jumped. He turned to Alvina with an ecstatic grin, but she had already begun walking back to the wagon by then.

Alvina stood in the shade of the barn for the next two hours. During this time, the small man showed Lawrence how to harness Rosie to the wagon and then unhook her. He then sold Lawrence two 20-gallon casks that each weighed over 160 pounds when full, several pounds of horse feed, a heavy washtub, lengths of rope, a shovel, and a small leather pouch of horseshoe nails "just in case."

By the time they at last rode back into town, Lawrence had agreed to give well over two hundred fifty dollars to the small man for all they were to buy. With a shake of the hand, the small man promised to have everything over to their inn by dusk the next day. Lawrence, in turn, promised he'd have the money ready. Alvina spent the rest of the day thinking a single thought again, like a mantra she believed might become true if said enough.

But I trust him. I do. I trust him. I do.

They had meant to go to bed early that night, to wake up well before the sun rose the next day. Still, that night, long after the oil lamp had been turned down to a flickering nub, Alvina lay awake, her cheek resting against Lawrence's shoulder. His chest rose and fell with a steady rhythm. She listened to the creaks of the old inn settling for the night. Somewhere down the hall, a floorboard groaned. A woman laughed softly below—probably one of the other guests saying goodnight. The sounds were ordinary, comforting in their simplicity. They would have none of them living alone in Medicine Bow, or Mule Creek, or wherever it was. They were to be the only people within five hundred acres.

"Are you asleep?" she whispered. After the deal had been struck, Alvina had resolved not to talk to Lawrence for the rest of the day, possibly longer. But now she felt her resolve collapsing under a new weight. Lawrence, surprised by Alvina's words, turned Alvina in bed.

"Not yet."

"You know we'll make it?"

"Know we'll make it where?"

"To wherever it is we're going. To a home. Something that will last."

He reached for her hand beneath the quilt.

"We've already made it this far. That's not nothing, is it?"

"But it's not a home yet. Not by a long shot."

"No," he agreed. "It's not. But it's a beginning."

They lay there for another long stretch, listening to the night breathe around them.

Eventually, Alvina whispered, "I'm not sure I'm ready."

"No one ever is."

The next morning, about an hour before the sun rose, they each resolved to take a bath. As she rinsed her body, Alvina thought of how this was likely the last real bath either of them would have for some time now. She slowly, methodically, cleaned every part she could get to, and did not rush herself one bit when Lawrence insisted that she was eating into his own bathing time, what with the wagon coming soon. She spent about half an hour cleaning herself, whereas he spent over five minutes.

Outside, the wind picked up and rustled the cottonwood leaves beyond the boarding house fence. Alvina saw the faintest of daylight begin to emerge as she finished dressing. She and Lawrence grabbed their trunks, settled their accounts with the innkeeper, and made their way outside to wait for their wagon and horse to arrive.

What if the horse gets sick? What if it dies? What if we can't find our markers? What if we run out of money before we even get the sod house built? What about the water? What if there is none on the property?

These and a thousand other seemingly obvious thoughts that had yet to cross Alvina's mind now whirred about there with such ferocity she could hardly straighten out before the next overran it.

Seeing the consternation in Alvina's face, Lawrence rested a hand on her shoulder.

"We'll figure it out. One thing at a time. One fencepost. One seed. One day."

Alvina smiled faintly at this, not because she felt reassured, but because she felt the necessity of believing as he did. After all, if there were any chance of making it out there, she'd have to accept.

A long silence followed before Lawrence added, "Tomorrow's the start of something, Alvina. Something I'd rather build with you more than anyone else."

A lump rose in her throat. "You always say the right thing."

But as Lawrence pointed out their big wagon in the distance, making its way towards the inn, Alvina thought of how there was nothing at all that could be said to make her feel better now. What were Lawrence's words of affirmation in comparison to the real threat of burglars, wildlife, disease, and everything else that would be out to get them both the moment they stepped on that wagon?

It took a minute for the small man to pull up beside them. Alvina noticed that the same wily grin from before was draped over his face now. He stopped the wagon before them, the horses kicking dust up in the faces of both the couple and alighted in a single jump. He shook each of their hands again and offered to help them pack the wagon. Alvina could only half listen as Lawrence told the man, in full detail, their plans for the ensuing weeks.

Chapter 12

They climbed up onto the wagon bench. Rosie snorted and pawed the earth once, ready. Once Lawrence had been satisfied that everything was secure enough in the wagon, he picked up the reins and used them as he'd been instructed the day before. The horse neighed, then began at a walking pace to drag the cart along. And with that, they rolled forward, the wagon creaking over the rutted lane, carrying them west.

As had been expected, the horse was too small and scrawny to pull such a wagon as had been expected; the couple made their way to the parcel about half as quickly as they would have liked. Not only did Rosie walk at a slower and more tiring pace, but Alvina frequently recommended they take breaks every two hours due to exhaustion. So it was that on the third day, the day they had been hoping to arrive at the parcel, they stopped in the tiny town, Buford, on the route, not even halfway there.

One inn, used by travelers like them, offered a warm room, bed, complimentary meal, horse feed, and even a guarded farm where two boys stood watch with pistols day and night. The price was steep, but the pair, eager for a real bed, accepted without hesitation.

That night, after stowing the horse and the wagon away, Alvina and Lawrence went to the dinner hall for their complimentary meal. They were given meager helpings of cornbread, beans, and salt-cured pork. Several families with noisy children ate alongside them in the dining room. All the parents looked exhausted. Lawrence and Alvina sat at a table for two in the corner without a window. They talked softly as they ate their meal, then quickly left for their room to get as much rest as they could.

The next morning, they were packed and ready in the dining room before the breakfast buffet opened. They wanted to beat the families and get on the road by sunrise, and they were successful in doing so. The wagon was on the trail by sunrise; but Rosie needed plenty of breaks, and soon the wagons of the other families from the inn began to pass them one by one.

"I told you we should've gone with one of the smaller wagons," Alvina said every so often when Rosie was let to rest again. Lawrence said nothing.

Resting or chugging along, the high prairie spread in every direction: dry grass, wild sage, and the occasional flicker of movement where a jackrabbit darted away. So too there were always several antelopes out in the distance. Alvina peered out over the prairie as they went.

"It all looks the same," she said. "Like we haven't moved at all."

Lawrence squinted toward the horizon.

"That's the West for you."

The next few days blended into one another much the same. After spending several nights in the covered wagon, they were pleased to spot the Virginian Hotel as they headed into Medicine Bow. Upon arrival, they unpacked a few essentials and some clean clothes, then let the workers take the wagon and Rosie to a safe place in the barn.

After each took a warm bath and changed clothes, Alvina and Lawrence were ready to head to the dining room for hot meal. An hour early for dinner, the pair went into the bar to kill the time.

Alvina had thought Lawrence and herself were the only two in the bar until, ten minutes after they had sat down on their stools, a tall woman a little older than herself walked up towards the pair and sat beside Alvina. The woman immediately introduced herself as Beth, and after a brief round of perfunctory small talk, the three began to really get talking.

Beth explained that she was a single woman who left the Midwest and homesteaded on her assigned parcel about a year ago. Excited to meet someone as experienced in frontier life as herself, Lawrence and Alvina soon barraged Beth with their many questions. In return, Beth told them about how she'd built her cabin by her lonesome when she first arrived and how she was now preparing for the winter. She told them how she had two horses and how, during the first winter, she had been forced to keep both in her cabin since she did not have a barn. She laughed at herself a great deal during this story, which somehow put Alvina at ease with the woman.

By the time the dining room opened, Beth suggested that they eat together. The pair excitedly consented, so that soon they were talking about Beth's weekly routine while they ate their pork. All throughout dinner, Alvina talked more freely; in turn,

Beth answered more and more of her questions with smiles and laughter of her own. Alvina was so relaxed by the end of the meal that she insisted Lawrence put Beth's dinner charge on their check.

After dinner, Beth told the couple she needed to leave to get back to her cabin before sunset. Right as she left, Alvina thought to ask Beth where she lived, so that they might meet up again if possible.

"Take the trail that goes north out of Medicine Bow for about 25 miles," Beth told her." When you get to Mule Creek, turn east. After a few miles you should see my cabin. It's the first one on Mule Creek, you can't miss it."

And with that, Beth thanked the pair for the dinner, said goodbye, and went on her way,

As she sat in bed in the hotel room, replaying the night's conversation over again, Alvina was surprised to see Lawrence putting on his boots again. She asked him if he was going out to check on Rosie, but he shook his head.

"After learning so much from Beth, I don't know if I'm ready to sleep. I think I might go get a drink and think about what that woman said for a bit. She certainly was nice, huh?"

He then asked Alvina if she'd like to come along with him, but now it was she who shook her head.

Though Alvina disliked the idea of being left alone, she felt too tired to go for drinks again. So, she let Lawrence go to the bar to relax a little, falling asleep quickly after he left.

"A man at the bar last night made it clear there is no chance of getting a job here in Medicine Bow. Said going to Mule Creek is the only way to find a high-paying job. Also told me what drinks are best out here, nothing like what you'd think to order in Indianapolis. He said…"

Alvina watched the seemingly infinite prairie span onward while half listening to Lawrence talk. It was the morning after now, and Lawrence had suggested that they go and try to find their parcel today. He had added that they could go back to the Virginian Hotel for one more comfortable bed and an excellent dinner if they couldn't find anything. Alvina secretly hoped this would be the case. Watching the prairie roll on, she was already thinking about what lay ahead: open campfires, tin cans of beans, and no bathrooms.

But it was not even noon yet when Alvina, keeping one eye on the compass, the other on the map, called out to Lawrence to stop the wagon. Beth gave perfect instructions to her cabin at the bar last night and again at dinner. Alvina was amazed that on the way to their parcel; they spotted Beth's cabin to the left.

"That's it," she said. "We're here."

He pulled gently on Rosie's reins, bringing the wagon to a slow halt. "You sure this is it?"

"We're on the southern edge of Beth's claim. The way she described it last night at the bar, our property line running south to north is the western edge of our parcel and eastern edge of her parcels. The lines touch. We are on the southern edge of Beth's property. Since her property is a square mile. If we ride one more mile we will be at our parcel. I'm sure of it."

She had been looking at the map for six days and six nights now. She was sure they were there.

As they approached the mile mark, Lawrence hopped down and began collecting stones, but he instantly saw the mile marker that Beth had made for her parcel. For six days and six nights, he had been telling Alvina how they would need to build such markers to know where their land began and ended.

"Let's make Beth's pile a bit bigger before we lose track. This'll be the first corner."

As Alvina began looking for stones, Lawrence spent the next half hour building a small tower of stones. Alvina took account of what provisions they had left, then surveyed the land. But there was so little to see; it looked much the same as everywhere else they'd been.

Once he was done with the first stone tower, the couple got back in the wagon and rode east. Lawrence urged Rosie forward again, doing his best to follow the invisible southern border.

"I'm guessing here," he admitted, "but the Claims Office said the mile markers were accurate enough for now."

They stopped again when Alvina spotted another pile of rocks in the distance.

"Looks like someone else had the same idea," she said.

Lawrence turned the wagon to the left and began heading north. This part of the drive proved even more challenging, with no tracks or ridges. Just grass and wind. Alvina kept checking the compass, squinting at the sun for guidance.

When they got to what they thought was the third corner of their land, Lawrence suggested they take a break and eat. So, after the wagon was once again brought to a stop, they got out and sat on the rocks, unwrapped their sandwiches, and shared a quiet meal: no toast, no silverware, no waiter in sight.

Alvina glanced around at the vast emptiness. An endless stretch of brown and gray dotted with sagebrush and the occasional jackrabbit darting by. She sighed and turned to Lawrence. He met her gaze and smiled as he chewed. She smiled back. That was enough. It had to be.

As they were sitting on the rocks, Lawrence recognized the man riding horseback down the trail. He stood up and called out.

"Hey, Paul! Over here! It's Lawrence, from the bar last night!"

The man evidently recognized Lawrence, as he stopped his horse shortly after Lawrence began yelling at him, dismounted and began walking towards the pair, leading the horse as he did so.

Lawrence said, "Alvina, this is Paul Miller. I met him last night at the bar. Paul, this is my wife, Alvina."

The man shook Alvina's hand. She noticed it was bruised and calloused all over.

"Paul was telling me about a job opportunity in Mule Creek that he thought I might consider. He and another man, Henry, are going to Mule Creek to get the details about the job. Paul, tell us where your parcel is around here. This here is ours."

Lawrence gestured to the land around them. Paul nodded.

"We're about one mile south of here. Right across the trail."

"Do you know Beth?" Alvina asked the man. "She lives right around here. She's our neighbor due West, actually."

The man shook his head.

"Never met her."

"Well, we met her yesterday," Alvina continued, undeterred. "She seems nice and on top of things. She is living out here all by herself. We had dinner with her at the Virginian."

Lawrence added, "She knows a lot about this area. She built her cabin all by herself apparently. Seemed like a nice and smart woman to us."

"Good to know," the man said, though Alvina thought she could sense a trace of dismissal in his tone. "Henry must live south of that woman. My family traveled with Henry and his wife and three children. We have known them for years back east."

Lawrence explained to Alvina that Henry was the name of the other man he had met at the bar the previous night.

"When are you thinking about leaving for Mule Creek?" Lawrence asked Paul.

"We were thinking of going late tomorrow afternoon. Keep in mind that Mule Creek is not a town. A start-up company is being built there on the prairie. They are hoping it will cultivate population growth. We heard that they were hiring."

"Would you mind if I join you?"

Before Alvina could say something, Paul answered Lawrence's question.

"Fine by me. Here, how about Henry and I meet you at this rock pile around noon tomorrow?"

"That'd be great! Thanks, Paul!" said Lawrence.

The man tipped his hat, then declared he'd better be on his way.

As soon as he was out of sight, Alvina hissed, "What you do think that you are doing? Are you going to dump me off tomorrow morning with a horse, wagon, water, and some food in the middle of nowhere? Did you think that you should at least ask me before planning in front of me?"

"Alvina, we are running out of money. I must find a job. Maybe you could walk over to Beth's cabin and stay while I am away. She seems like a nice woman."

The two argued over the matter awhile until Lawrence declared they should go back to the Virginian hotel. This confused Alvina.

"I thought we weren't going back. We found our land, didn't we?"

Lawrence shrugged. He thought that he would ride back to this location to meet the men tomorrow.

"You're impossible, you know that? I know how much you'd prefer to be sleeping back there than here. So, let's go back to the Virginian and have a last good dinner. We'll talk all this over in the room. I promise."

Lawrence signaled the end of the conversation by signaling the reigns for Rosie. Alvina reluctantly let the matter be too relieved by the return to the hotel to further press Lawrence for the time being.

Chapter 13

But despite Lawrence's promise, no such conversation about his plans were discussed that night. Alvina lay down as soon as they got back and accidentally fell asleep even before eating dinner. By the time she woke, it was the next morning, and Lawrence was packing their things, preparing to leave.

"Lawrence, what happened?" she asked in a dazed confusion.

"You fell asleep as soon as we got back."

"Why didn't you wake me? God, I didn't even eat dinner last night."

Lawrence shrugged.

"You looked like you needed the sleep. Figured you wouldn't have wanted me to wake you. Here," he said, handing her one of their satchels, "you pack everything else up for me. I need to go check us out and get Rosie."

Groggy and disoriented by the situation, Alvina forgot of the talk the two were supposed to have the previous night. Instead, she spent a few minutes left in the hotel stumbling about the room, trying to shake off her sleepiness while she packed.

So too did Alvina completely forget what lay in store for them that day, so that when a wagon began approaching the pair, who had arrived at their property only an hour earlier, she grew confused and anxiously pointed it out to Lawrence. It was only when she saw the face of Paul did, she remember everything.

As planned, Paul and Henry had arrived close to noon to pick Lawrence up in one of their wagons. To Alvina's surprise, however, the wives and children of the two men also came along in two wagons. One of them jumped off the wagon as soon as the men did, introducing herself first to Alvina. Her name was Penny.

"Don't you worry, dear," the woman said with a warm, reassuring smile on her face. "My husband told us how you two were all alone out here. I said to him 'So she's going to be left out there, by herself, with nothing but a wagon?' I swear sometimes these men do their best to avoid thinking at all costs." She shot an aggressive but playful look towards Paul. "So, I told them we'd come and bring you over to our cabin instead. You can stay there while the men are away."

"And we'll come back a little later to take your wagon and horse to our cabin," Penny said, "that way no one will steal it. Better yet, we can take it now. Do you think that you can manage your horse if we go slow?"

"Yes, I have never tried but I will try now."

A wave of relief washed over Alvina as she returned the woman's smile as best as she could.

"I was afraid of being alone out here," she admitted. "I'm glad you came. I will try to turn our wagon around, if I can."

"Take it slow. We are not in any rush."

Alvina's hands were shaking, but she managed to get Rosie walking enough to turn the wagon. After a few yards, she felt somewhat comfortable.

By then, the three men had already gotten in the other wagon, where they were talking about the journey ahead. Alvina didn't have time to watch their wagon disappear in the distance.

Alvina nodded and managed to follow the Penny's wagon, feeling a mixture of relief and dazedness. Who were these people she was suddenly following off into the unknown with? And yet it was better than being out here all alone.

Alvina was so focused that she was surprised when Penny pulled over for a rest stop at the halfway mark.

As the wagon unloaded, Alvina saw the other man's wife, as well as several of the children, that had come along in the wagon, too. Each introduced themselves, then began bombarding her with questions. Alvina soon realized how rare a thing it must've been to meet someone new out here on the frontier. She was relieved when Penny took hold on the conversation at last.

"We've known each other since Ohio. It's been nearly five years now. Our husbands came out here full of schemes about free land and big skies." She sighed, half-smiling. "They were more interested in homesteading than we were."

The other wife, Lillian, snorted at this.

"That's putting it mild. Henry dragged me out here, and we're still sleeping in a wagon with Ruthie. Imagine that—with a toddler!"

The toddler was the only child Henry and Lillian had, or so Alvina gathered. It was Paul and Penny, the man she'd met yesterday and his gregarious wife she was meeting today, that had had enough kids to fill the wagon to the brim. A pair of pre-adolescent twin sons, Tommy and Jacob, an older teenage daughter, Millie, and a collie named Scout made up their bunch. Alvina was simultaneously relieved and overwhelmed by their company.

"Meanwhile, they built one big cabin for Penny's family and a single outhouse for the lot of us."

"One outhouse?" Alvina blinked.

"Exactly," Penny replied, rolling her eyes. "You'd think they were building a palace instead of four walls and a roof."

The wives laughed together, the sharp edge of their shared frustration softening into camaraderie. Though she didn't laugh at the comment, a small smile came over Alvina unconsciously. For the first time since Lawrence had spoken of the homestead, Alvina felt she wasn't the only one questioning the men's plans.

"Have you met Beth yet?" Alvina asked.

"Who?" Penny asked. Alvina told her and the rest in the wagon what she had told Paul the day before.

"She's capable," Alvina explained. "Already has her own cabin, an outhouse, and starting to build a barn for her two horses. She told me she'd lend us a hand building. Honestly, Lawrence doesn't know a hammer from a saw."

Lillian chuckled. "Sounds like Paul. He can recite Shakespeare better than he can drive a nail straight."

Soon, everyone piled back into the wagon and Alvina resumed her driver seat for the second half of the ride.

The cabin was easy to spot as they neared Penny's place, a lone outpost rising from the vast, empty prairie. Its sturdy logs were neatly split and stacked, the roof shingled at a slight slope to shed the snow, with two modest windows catching the last of the sun. A single outhouse stood at the edge of the yard, with a clothesline strung between it and the cabin's front corner, now heavy with drying garments flapping in the wind. From the roof a crooked pipe, carrying smoke from the wood-burning stove that promised both warmth and food.

Inside, the cabin glowed with the steady heat of that stove, the air wrapping around them like a soft quilt. The women moved with practiced rhythm—Penny's hands kneading dough with swift, sure strokes before dropping biscuits into a sizzling iron pan, while Lillian balanced Ruthie on one hip and ladled steaming soup into bowls. The rich scent of onions, beans, and herbs filled the cramped space, reminding everyone of comfort despite the harshness outside.

The Sanders' small bedroom was large enough for the parents' bed, while the three children slept in the main room on cots layered with handmade quilts and feather pillows. Along one wall, shelves offered a touch of homely pride: a stack of worn board games, a few classic books, and wooden puzzles polished by years of small, eager hands. Even in the middle of the raw prairie, the cabin felt alive—more than timber and nails, it was a place of warmth, laughter, and stubborn hope.

The children huddled together after supper, spread across the floor with a well-worn checkerboard and a few homemade game pieces. Their laughter echoed off the log walls until, one by one, they drifted toward sleep on quilts and makeshift pallets.

When the last giggle faded and the final spoon was dried and placed neatly on the shelf, the cabin quieted. The three women gathered near the dim light of the stove, voices low, as if the darkness outside might be listening.

Penny broke the silence first. "Our savings are slipping through our fingers quicker than I ever imagined. Henry thought the land would feed us faster."

Lillian sighed, rubbing her forehead. "Same with Paul and me. We thought we had planned carefully, but the bills pile up faster than the crops grow. It's worse than Ohio in some ways."

Alvina's heart pounded. She leaned forward, her voice sharp with sudden panic. "We've only been here a few days, and I already see our money vanishing. I thought it was just me—just us—being careless."

Lillian shook her head. "No. It's all of us. That's why the men are talking about jobs in Laramie. It pays steady."

Her tone carried no relief, only resignation. Alvina froze.

"In Laramie? I thought they were going to Mule Creek?"

"They always say that, but they know as well as we do, they pass through there for the food. One family makes great barbeque outside their place there, but that's all. If there's no jobs in Medicine Bow, there's even less in Mule Creek. No, they're headed for Laramie."

"But isn't that almost a hundred miles away?"

"One hundred and seven!" Lillian said sharply. Alvina felt heaviness in her chest developing but not wanting to make herself a burden on the others she did her best to appear nonplussed by this new information.

"And what kind of jobs would they be looking for?"

"They didn't say much—railroad and the power company work, maybe," Penny said carefully.

"How do they plan on going there every day though? It's too far for that," Alvina said perplexedly. Penny's face dropped at this comment, realizing what it was she'd have to tell Alvina.

"Dear, they don't go there and back every day. Any job in Laramie they take, they're going to have to find a place to stay there during the weekdays."

"Henry said they might not come back for as much as three weeks at a time," Lillian added casually as she worked. The words struck Alvina with such force she had to sit down to catch herself.

"Three weeks? Lawrence didn't tell me anything about being away that long. Not even for a week at a time, let alone three weeks."

Lillian let out a bitter laugh. "That's not what Paul said, either. But you know how men are. Sometimes you got to wrangle stuff out of them."

The casualness of Lillian's comment, in the face of the monumental shift Alvina's life was taking, made Alvina nauseous. She hunched over herself and closed her eyes. Soon a woman's hand began to rub her back gently.

"Hey, they might not even get those jobs." It was Penny who was speaking, trying to console her. "And if they do, you won't be alone. We'll be here, too. If the men are gone, we'll have to hold this place together ourselves."

For a moment, Alvina felt the walls close in on this cabin, this prairie, this future that seemed less like a dream and more like a trap. When had she fallen into it? Could she ever get out? But the nausea overwhelmed her to the point that even these questions were pushed away.

"We'll survive," Penny said softly as she continued to rub Alvina's back, with more determination than certainty. "Because we'll do it together."

Alvina swallowed hard, whispering, "Yes, yes."

The men did not return for several days. During this time, Alvina became more accustomed to the Sanders' cabin and its inhabitants. She began to even count herself lucky, all things considered. These two families she had so randomly met, who Lawrence had so haphazardly entrusted her entire safety with, turned out to be some of the nicest people she had ever met. The wives were kind and motherly, while the kids were rambunctious but well-mannered when necessary. To repay the families for their hospitality, Alvina did all that she could to help around the cabin. This included, two days after the husbands left, going into Medicine Bow to help shop for supplies.

The ride to the town was nothing of note, any more than Alvina and Lawrence's ride back to the Virginia Hotel had been a few days earlier. The shopping proved brisk and unnoteworthy as well, as the two wives had gotten its routine down to such a science that Alvina could only help pack the heavier things into the wagon without getting in the way of the two women. It was on the ride home that something out of the ordinary occurred.

The wagon had been passing by the Virginia Hotel on its way out of town when the wagon came to a halt. Alvina had been watching the building pass by longingly, but even she was surprised when the wagon came to a halt before it passed into the distance.

"Did you see that sign on the hotel window?" Penny said to Lillian, pointing to one of the hotel's windows. "HELP WANTED. We should check it out."

Before Lillian or Alvina could object, Penny had jumped out of the wagon and began heading towards the hotel's entrance on foot. She hadn't even thought to tie the horses to a post before heading into the hotel alone.

"What do you think the job is?" Alvina said as she watched Lillian get out of the vehicle and lead the wagon to the nearest post.

"Probably washing sheets and the like. Maybe barmaid, but probably not," Lillian guessed.

"You think she'd want us to work there? I've never worked in a hotel before. Only a freight company. I don't know if I could do something like that."

Lillian shrugged.

"I doubt it'd be something too hard."

Once the wagon was tied, Lillian got back in the wagon. She and Alvina chatted idly for a little while before Penny came back from the hotel. A wide grin on her face told them all they needed to know.

"We're hired," she said cheerfully as she hopped into the wagon.

"Hired?" Even Lillian was stunned by this comment. "I don't even know what the job is yet."

"They need people to clean rooms and wash linens—seven days a week, about four or five hours a day."

"What about the children?" Alvina felt the full irony of her asking this question, but someone had to. Penny waved her hand.

"They can play outside here or stay at home. They're getting to be old enough to take care of themselves."

This was true of Penny's children, who were around eleven and seventeen, respectively. But Lillian's child was still a toddler. Perhaps recognizing this, Penny's oldest daughter, who had also come along on the errand trip, spoke up.

"I can watch Ruthie," she suggested.

"Oh, I wouldn't make you do that," Lillian said. "I couldn't make you do that."

"I'd rather do that than do nothing."

"They didn't even meet us," Alvina interjected. "How are they already willing to hire us?"

"They're desperate, I guess."

Penny whipped on the reins and began heading the wagon out of town. Alvina began to argue they should go back, that they couldn't be hired for a job without at least talking to their employer, but Penny refused, saying it was already too late in the day for them to be in town any longer.

Penny eagerly talked of the job as they began their way back, but after almost every sentence, she was interrupted by qualms from the other two women.

"I can't leave Ruthie, Penny. You know I can't."

"I took us from flat broke to seven dollars a week!" Penny said, with the faintest note of contempt in her voice. "If you two really want to turn that down to twiddle your thumbs for weeks at a time, waiting for our husbands to get back, be my guest. I can't do that."

Alvina said. "Laramie's not that far. They said they'd be back in a few days, too. Besides, they haven't found a job yet anyway. They might not find any jobs there."

Penny snorted at this, and soon a hush fell over the wagon for the rest of the trip back. Alvina realized the others were considering the jobs in Laramie much more of a sure thing than she had.

Discussion among the three women didn't start up again until deep into the night, when the children were asleep in the cabin. The women had gathered around the table once dinner was finished and the pots and pans cleaned. They poured small shots of whiskey to relax.

It was Penny who began the conversation.

"Alright," she said in a calm, measured tone, "are you two ready to discuss the work?"

Alvina groaned.

"Can't it wait until tomorrow? A lot has happened today already. I'm exhausted."

And she was, physically as well as emotionally tired. The wagon trip had reminded her of Lawrence's betrayal, and all the feelings of anger, frustration, resentment, and despair she had slowly let go of the past few days had come rushing back to her on the ride home. Now she desired the oblivion of sleep above all else. But Penny was not willing to let her have this, shaking her head firmly at Alvina's request.

"This conversation can't wait. The hotel is expecting us tomorrow."

"Penny, they're expecting *you,*" Alvina countered. "They haven't even met us."

"And I can't have your daughter watch the baby," Lillian added. "It was sweet of her to offer, but she's still a kid herself. Not an adult."

"Hold on, hold on. Alvina, Lillian, I've been thinking about this a lot since we got back. I need you two to listen to my plan before you say anything more. Please."

She took their momentary silence as a sign of approval and continued.

"You were right to say what you did, Lillian. We need an adult watching our kids out here, I've come to realize. I was a bit too eager when I heard of the job, but I've thought it through more now. And Alvina, you were right when you said they're only expecting me tomorrow. And I think it would be best if I went tomorrow. That means you two will have to keep an eye on Millie, Tommy, Jacob, and Ruthie. And, of course, Scout, too."

"So, what, we're going to watch your kids every day while you work?" Lillian's voice was more charged now than Alvina had ever heard it before.

"I wouldn't make you do that," Penny said, maintaining the calm tone she'd began with. "Look, one of us is going to have to stay here with the kids, no matter what. That much is a given. But what if only one of us, or two at the most, go and work at the hotel each day while the others stay back?"

"The hotel wouldn't let us do that," Alvina said. She thought back to her freight job and how girls had gotten fired there for trying to foist shifts off onto other co-workers.

"I think they would. You weren't there to see it, but those people are so desperate for help that they'd hire anyone. So, I was thinking, I will go tomorrow and see what they think about this. Propose to them what I'm saying to you all now. If they're alright with only one or two of us coming in each day, then maybe on the second day, you two could go together. Neither of you has much experience handling the horse and wagon, and it'd be safer for you to travel as a pair."

Alvina and Lillian exchanged a look. Penny began to say something more but was interrupted by a cry from Ruthie.

"Look, think it over tonight. That's all I'm asking."

Lillian was rocking Ruthie back to sleep when she said, "Alvina, I imagine you're as tired as I am. Let's talk about this tomorrow while she's at work."

Penny shuffled off to bed shortly after this, with Lillian leaving moments after her. This left Alvina alone at the table to think of all that had happened. Why couldn't the men work at the hotel? Why was it such a sure thing they were going to work in Laramie? Had Lawrence really known they had planned to go to Laramie for work the whole time, or had he thought they were only going to Mule Creek, like he'd told her? Did that even matter now? And how long could she stay here with these women if he did go to Laramie? Indefinitely? It didn't seem they'd ever force her out, but was this what she wanted?

Dozens of questions continued to rush through Alvina's mind as she sat at the table looking off into space. However, two questions kept coming back to her, repeatedly. How did she get here, and where was she headed?

Chapter 14

It was mid-afternoon when Penny got home from her first day of hotel cleaning. She was anxious to share that the hotel owner, Mrs. Evans, agreed to have Alvina and Lillian work as a team, as well as to let the pair sync their working days with those Penny took off.

"So, what do you think?" Penny asked expectantly after explaining the situation to the two women. The three were gathered in the living room, close to the fireplace.

Alvina looked towards Lillian. The two had been discussing this possibility all day.

Lillian clapped her hands softly. "That should be a dollar a day between us two, right?"

"That's right!" Penny said.

"And we won't have to find a sitter for the children, either?" Alvina added.

Penny nodded.

"I think we can't turn something like this down, can we, Alvina?" Lillian said.

Before Alvina could answer, Penny was up on her feet, excitedly talking about all the things their new wages could buy them. Axes. Plows. Flour. Pans. Sewing tools. Iodine. Kerosene. Maybe even a nice cast-iron stove, if they save up.

Though she almost missed it, Alvina saw the shadow of a smile come over Lillian. A weight lifted now from her chest, too. The plan was settled, so that now the only thing they could do was let the warmth of the fire soak into their bones before starting dinner. For the first time since arriving, it felt like they had a plan.

It was around six o'clock that day one of the Millers' boys ran inside, yelling "There's Dad now!" It took less than a minute for the whole cabin to empty outside.

The women shaded their eyes and exchanged relieved glances as their wagon approached.

The men climbed down stiffly once the wagon came to a stop. Their clothes were dusty and their faces weary. Lawrence was the first to speak.

"We're all starving."

Alvina noticed he was averting his gaze from her as he talked, looking towards the other women instead. She stepped directly in front of him, looking him straight in the eye as she did so.

"We need to talk."

"After dinner," Lawrence said, placing a hand on her shoulder. She shrugged it off.

"Not after dinner. Now."

Lawrence let out an exasperated sigh but followed Alvina as she motioned him away from the rest of the reuniting crowd.

"If you expect to eat dinner before explaining why you lied to me about your job, you're sorely mistaken. Penny and Lillian said that their husbands told them, *before they left*, that they knew a job in Laramie would mean being away for weeks at a time. You knew that too, didn't you? Why didn't you tell me?"

"I didn't want to upset you. Besides, the guys in the bar said they would put a good word in for us at the power company. Sure, they might have told us about being gone for weeks at a time, but then they never promised we would get hired, either."

Alvina saw Lawrence look at the ground as he talked. It frustrated her even more.

"No, you didn't want me to forbid you to go, like I ought to have. You knew I wouldn't have let you go if you told me all that, so you decided not to tell me at all."

Alvina waited for Lawrence to respond. He kept looking at the ground as he spoke.

"We need money. This job pays well. I thought you would like it if I found something that brought in a steady income."

She dismissed his comment and continued.

"And now you accepted a job that leaves me alone on this god forsaken wasteland for three weeks each month. Is that your plan?"

"We have to make sacrifices to survive out here."

Alvina scoffed at this. "Thank God for Penny and Lillian, or else it'd be the same as if you'd deserted me out here. Thank God we all got jobs, or I would've died of boredom."

Lawrence looked up.

"Jobs? You shouldn't need a job with the money I'll make working in Laramie. That's the whole reason the men and I did this, so that you all could work on the homestead for us."

"What did you say? 'So that the women can work on the homestead for you?' Did you ask the women if that's what they wanted to do, or did you decide that for them while you were out in Laramie?"

"You should quit," Lawrence said sternly, trying to keep hold of the conversation as best he could. Alvina shook her head.

"You didn't even give me the chance to talk to you about your new job. Why should I talk to you at all about mine?"

"Because we're married."

Alvina laughed derisively at this.

"Little good that's done me so far," she said nastily. "Now you're starting to see how I felt."

She looked Lawrence in the face, who at last was returning her gaze in full sincerity. She wondered where that man she'd married less than a year ago had gone. He hadn't been like this before, had he? Not on their wedding day, at least. Not in the letters. But then, what if she had seen something that wasn't there? Had she really let herself been dragged this far west by a man who now looked more stranger than husband, more burden than partner?

Alvina let out a deep sigh.

"I'm going to go help with dinner while you get washed and changed." She walked away.

The other men had finished washing up by the time Alvina returned to Penny's cabin. They were sitting around the table, talking to their wives about their time in Laramie.

"You're never going to believe the day we had," Henry began. "One of the longest ones I've had since we left home, and that's saying something."

"We started by looking for the power company the guys in Medicine Bow told us about." Paul chimed in. "Figured that was a sure thing."

"But their building was harder to find than expected. They didn't have a big sign posted outside like most companies back home," Henry continued. "Then, when we finally did find it, we walked in as a manager was heading to lunch. We asked whether they were hiring, and he told us they were, but that we'd have to sit and wait until he came back from lunch before he could interview any of us. Well, we sat there for two hours, wondering if we'd made a mistake."

Alvina laughed derisively, so that one of the men looked at her briefly before continuing with their story. After Lawrence's lies, Alvina found herself doubting the truth of what these men said, too. She felt more inclined to believe they had got the jobs the moment they walked into the power company, then spent the rest of their trip at the Laramie bars. After all, how hard had it been for them three women to find work?

Henry began to speak again a couple of moments after Alvina's interruption.

"And when we were about ready to give up and head out, they called us in. One by one."

"What did they offer?" one of the children asked.

"A good wage. Better than we expected."

"Unfortunately, it's like those guys at the bar told us how it'd be. The power company is going to require us to work six days a week for three straight weeks, like they said. Then we'll get five days off before the next cycle. Of course, we'll try and come home every break we get."

Alvina had to fight not to laugh at this, too, restraining herself at the last second. They'd *try?* Could they not even promise to see them once a month?

"At least we've got jobs now," Henry said.

"That wasn't even the worst part of it all, either," Paul said, grinning as he did so. "That night, after the interview, they only had one room left at the boardinghouse we stayed at. So, there we were—two of us squeezed into a bed. Poor Lawrence had to sleep on the floor!"

The two men burst out laughing heartily, as did the two Sanders' boys. But their laughter was quickly cut short by a snort from Alvina.

"That cannot be the worst part of your trip," she said, snappily. "The worst part was leaving us women and children to fend for ourselves. But then again it was probably good you all did that, so now we'll know what three out of four weeks of the rest of our lives are going to be like from here on out."

Silence fell in the cabin. Alvina stood for a moment, waiting for a response. When none came, she retired into their covered wagon.

Alvina did not leave the covered wagon all night, even when the coyotes began to howl. She swayed in and out of sleep until the next morning. The only thing she remembered from the rest of the night was Lawrence's hand suddenly grabbing hers and squeezing it tight as he lay down beside her.

"We'll make it work," he promised. "One way or another, we'll make this a home."

She pretended to be asleep.

Chapter 15

The Miller's toddler, Ruthie, ran a bad fever the next morning, so Lillian said she'd be unable to cover her shift that day. Penny volunteered to take care of the toddler while Lillian went into town. When that approach failed, Penny volunteered to go with Alvina to town, but Alvina shook her head firmly, saying there was no need for concern. She left the cabin half an hour before the time Penny had recommended, and before Lawrence woke up. It was the men's last day before they'd have to return to Laramie.

By now, Alvina could handle a horse and wagon to go into town alone. The Sanders' wagon and horse were different from riding with Rosie, but soon she found the change enjoyable. The horse did not need to frequently stop like Rosie did, and ran faster when it went, so Alvina could now feel a wind against her face even when there was none.

The work proved enjoyable as well and she liked the change of setting, too. During her time in the cabin so far, Alvina found herself constantly seeking to help with work. While the women appreciated the extra pair of hands, they had long learned how to tend to all the work themselves. Because of this, most of the chores they assigned to Alvina so far had been menial. Cleaning the hotel rooms by herself, she had at last had a sense of making a significant contribution to something, especially because she was being paid.

The men were gone by the time Alvina got home from her work at the hotel. Penny rushed up to her as she entered the cabin, peppering her with questions as to how her work at the hotel had gone. The two talked for about an hour before Alvina noticed someone was missing.

"Where's Lillian and her baby?"

Penny's expression, which had been cheerful as could be until then, tightened a bit as her smile receded and her eyes narrowed.

"Lillian started feeling bad herself after you left. Her husband decided it was best to have them come with them to Laramie to see a doctor. They left with the men a few hours ago."

Penny tried to force a smile when she saw the concern in Alvina's expression.

"Oh, it'll be alright. They're being extra careful is all – you must be, out here on the frontier. The men said one of us could bring them back after our shifts in a few days if everything turns out fine, which I'm sure it will. Don't you worry about it."

She patted Alvina's outstretched hand gently.

"I'm going to need your help a lot more now, after all. Penny can help too, but I'm going to need you to fill in for a good amount of the work Lillian did. Think you can handle that?"

Alvina chuckled gently and said she'd do her best.

The two women alternated days working at the hotel for the rest of the week. As Penny had said, Alvina needed to fill in for the great number of tasks Lillian left behind. Feelings of being unproductive and in the way left her. By the end of Lillian's first day away, she felt no emotion besides exhaustion. Penny did her best to help Alvina, but it was clear Alvina would now have to spend nearly every waking hour doing some tasks. How Lillian had done all this work, she could not imagine. And so it was that, when Alvina began to be short of breath and have fleeting fits of nausea, she wrote off the symptoms as that of general exhaustion.

Still, Alvina worked on. Sometimes, when she had a moment to think, Alvina found satisfaction in her fatigue. At times she was even proud of being short of breath and nauseous, believing it to be a testament to how hard she was working. She had thought she was doing a good job of concealing these symptoms, too, until Penny confronted her one morning before work.

"Alvina, you're not going into work today."

Alvina had been organizing her things in the early morning when Penny said this to her, so she jumped a little in surprise.

"Why not? Today's my day to go in, isn't it?"

"It is, but you're not going in all the same. You're pale as a ghost right now, you know that?"

Alvina blushed at this.

"I'm always a little fainter in the morning. I'll be alright once I get there."

"You napped all of yesterday afternoon."

"I needed the sleep."

Penny eyed her skeptically.

"You were out to the outhouse almost an hour after that, too."

"The food –" Alvina began before stopping herself. She had been nauseous to the point of thinking she was going to vomit yesterday, but she hadn't and so wrote the experience off as a strange one-off. It was only now when Penny presented all the pieces to her in succession did Alvina see the big picture,

"Maybe I'm coming down with a cold. The smell of food cooking does me nauseous."

Penny looked at her skeptically.

"Dear, with all the kids here, I'd prefer it if we were cautious about these things."

"Penny, I'm fine. It's a cold, if anything at all." Yet now that she had spoken it into existence, she thought of Lillian and Ruth, and how they had not come back yet.

"I'd prefer it if you get checked up on, just to be safe."

"But there's no doctors in town, are there? Or else wouldn't Lillian and Ruth have gone there instead of Laramie? And you can't possibly take me to Laramie – what about the kids?"

"I am thinking about the kids," Penny said, in what Alvina thought was the grimmest she had ever heard her voice. For a moment, the two stared at each other in the eyes, a standoff Alvina had hardly known she was in until a moment ago, much less what to do. Then an idea came to her.

"Here, if you don't want me going into work, I have another place you can take me."

Despite being home to only one person, the cabin Penny pulled to a stop at was significantly bigger. It also looked significantly more well-built, Alvina noted. But that was all she had time to note before Penny knocked on the door. To their relief, a woman opened the door.

"Beth," said Alvina, "do you remember me?"

Beth did not respond with words but instead stepped through the door frame and hugged Alvina.

"I was worried about you!" She said with emotion in her voice. "I went over to your land the other day and no one was there. Half of me thought you all had left for home, and the other half thought you must've been killed or something out here."

Alvina broke free of the hug.

"No, there are two families here. They've been kind enough to take us in until we get enough money to try and build our cabin."

She gestured to Penny, who waved.

"I've been with them the past couple weeks. But something's come up and I was wondering if you could take me to a doctor. Penny here has three kids back home to take care of and can't possibly put me in a wagon and take me back to Laramie."

Beth looked at Alvina inquisitively.

"There's a doctor in Medicine Bow one day each week. That's much closer than Laramie. But here," she stepped past Alvina, towards the wagon. She grabbed the large bundle of Alvina's immediate belongings from the wagon. "You come on inside and let Mrs. Penny get back to her kids while we talk this all over."

Alvina looked at Penny, whose welcoming smile she took as her cue to say good-bye. The two women hugged, Alvina told Penny to give her best to the kids, and the woman was off.

"She's a piece of work, huh?" Beth said as she watched the wagon ride off.

"What?"

"Never mind. Here, come on in."

The inside of Beth's cabin was even more aesthetically pleasing than the outside. There were photos on the walls, the smell of incense burning somewhere permeated through the house, and you could easily walk through the house without fear of bumping into this or that piece of cramped furniture. Alvina looked on in admiration as she sat down on one of the two firm wicker chairs. She was most impressed by the sense of someone human living here, enjoying their time here and making it a home for themselves, rather than simply trying to survive in it.

"Now, tell me about this sickness," Beth said as she sat beside Alvina. When Alvina finished listing her symptoms, Beth gave her a half-smile.

"I'm afraid you have the worst sickness of them all," she said, her voice a little higher than usual. But Alvina was by then too tense for jokes.

"What is it? Beth, please tell me. I've been so worried about it the whole ride over, and now Penny must think it's something bad or she wouldn't have sent me here, would she? Oh God, please tell me what it is so I can stop all this worrying."

Beth offered a gentle smile and said, "Is there any chance that you could be pregnant?"

"Pregnant?" Alvina made no effort to hide her astonishment. "Well, we have been so busy working at the hotel, it never crossed my mind. But I haven't, we haven't…"

Beth picked up the conversation for Alvina.

"Sometimes it takes months for you to know."

"Oh, wouldn't Lawrence be surprised. He comes home and sees me all big and pregnant the next time he gets back. But do you really think it's so?"

Beth shrugged.

"We can still go and try to see the doctor in Medicine Bow if you want. But I'd bet half of everything I have that he tells you what I did. It's up to you."

Alvina smiled with a bit of embarrassment.

"No, I don't think we'll need to do that. Your summary of my symptoms makes sense." Alvina let out a sigh. "Do you happen to have any tea? I'm feeling a little rattled by all this."

"Of course!" Beth stood up and patted Alvina's thigh gently. "You stay here and settle in. I'll be back in a bit."

Alvina smiled and nodded, then surveyed the house as she sat alone. Its homeliness reminded her much more of the homes she'd left in Indianapolis than those she'd seen on the frontier so far.

Beth returned with two small cups of warm tea some ten minutes later. After a few sips, Alvina found it in herself to speak again.

"Is there anything I should do, if I really am pregnant?"

Beth smiled.

"Not for a few months at least. All you can do now is be careful to not trip and fall or work too much if you can avoid it."

"But I can't avoid it!" Alvina couldn't contain herself. "Lawrence and I have so much to do to get done before winter. Beth, I can't have a baby, not now –"

"Calm down, calm down Alvina. They say stress is bad for a baby. For right now if you can try and forget about all that's going to happen."

"But I can't! I can't forget about myself or Lawrence. I especially can't forget about this new mouth we're going to have to feed, when we can barely feed ourselves."

"Then how about we don't talk about you? Let's talk about something else."

Alvina nodded empathically at the suggestion.

"How about we talk about you instead?" Alvina said. "You told us about yourself at the hotel when we first met, but that was all homestead and frontier stories. I'm sick of all that. How about you tell me about your life before you came here?"

"My life before I came here?" Beth echoed. "I haven't talked about any of that since God knows when. Since I first came here, probably."

"Well what better time to talk about it than now?" Alvina wheedled. "Please, Beth. I'd like to think of anyone else's troubles beside my own right now. Please."

Beth eyed her suspiciously but let out a sigh of assent.

"Well, I don't really know where to start."

"How about when you were eighteen or nineteen? That's about the age I first left home."

Beth laughed a little.

"When I was eighteen years old, I thought I'd fallen in love."

"Why are you laughing?" Alvina said.

"Because I didn't know what love was. I thought I'd fallen in love without once knowing what it was like to have a loving family. It's not that I hate my parents – they never hit me like I know some others do. But I wouldn't call them loving, either. More like always exhausted, and always complaining."

"I'm sorry to hear that," Alvina said as she helped herself to another cup of tea. For the first time in many months, she thought of her mother and her childhood home. Beth shrugged.

"It's how it was. So yes, at eighteen I was working in a cafe in Iowa, and I was in love."

"Then what?" Alvina asked, knowing the romance couldn't have ended well.

"We moved in together at eighteen to get away from our homes. I met him working at a café, and we moved in three months after I started the job. He talked to me of moving to New York and getting married there. He said his uncle was some big financier there and that he'd work for him while I made us a home."

"But you two never made it to New York?"

"He might have. One day, I came home to our apartment and found he wasn't there. Neither were his belongings, and neither was either of our money."

Alvina began to apologize.

"Don't apologize," Beth cut her off. "I deserved it. I was young and naïve and thought good of everyone. That's what happens to people like that. They get taken advantage of."

"So you went back to your parents?"

Beth shook her head.

"I would've starved before doing that. No, I scraped by as best I could, and when I couldn't I became a prostitute."

"A prostitute?" The word repulsed Alvina to think of, let alone say. And yet the woman before her now had declared herself one, declared herself a *prostitute,* as though it was the same as being a waitress or from Cincinnati.

"A prostitute?" Alvina repeated. Beth smiled, amused by Alvina's response.

"It wasn't too hard a racket. I knew another girl at the café who did that kind of stuff at night, so the week rent was due I asked her about it and she helped me out."

"Helped you out?" Though Alvina made no effort to hide how much the idea repulsed her, Beth continued to smile slyly.

"We worked together a while. Funniest thing about it all was that the man who sought me out most was the cafe chef!" Beth laughed. "Then when I told him I wasn't making enough money and would probably have to go home soon, he said *he* would marry me!" She laughed even harder at this.

"And you two did get married?"

Beth nodded.

"First I wanted to get married and then didn't, and then I didn't want to get married and did."

"At least you didn't have to go home then."

"I wish I would've gone home," Beth responded. "At home I didn't get beat. You see this?" She pointed to underneath her eye, where Alvina now saw a small dent she hadn't noticed before.

"I'm sorry," Alvina said, not knowing what else there was to say.

"It's alright. I lived. You know, a lot of the time he'd tell me he was beating me for being a whore, and I'd tell him if I hadn't been a whore, we'd have never meet in the first place. Then he'd beat me more for telling him that."

"How did you get out of that?" Alvina asked, wanting to move on to the next chapter of Beth's life as quickly as possible. The idea of the woman before her being bloodied and bruised made her cringe, and now she couldn't stop picturing it.

"I tolerated the situation as best I could. When I finally realized I was going to be beaten to death if I stayed with him much longer, I tried working the streets again. Then he found out about that and took the money I made and nearly did beat me to death. I couldn't get out of bed for three days after that.

Finally, I got smart and realized I'd already been given the answer on what to do long ago."

"The answer?"

Beth only smiled.

"I waited for spring. Then I got him really drunk one clear afternoon. When he passed out on the floor, I was already packed and ready to go. I left with one satchel bag and the latch box I knew he kept underneath one of the floorboards beneath the bed. By the time he woke up, I must've already been on the train to Cheyenne. For a couple of months prior, I had been reading about homesteading in Wyoming in the newspapers. There's the one thing I regret about it all, not being there to see his face when he realized it was all up. That and not leaving any earlier, I guess. "

Alvina thought of the dozens of newspapers Lawrence had shown her. She wondered if any of these papers had been the same ones that moved Beth to make her way west as well. She watched the woman across from her calmly sip her tea and found herself wondering how someone could go through such a gauntlet of a life and come out the other side laughing. Alvina found herself confused, impressed, and even slightly scared of this woman she had thought was so simple previously.

"And then you came here?" Alvina said.

"And then I came here." Beth nodded. The two were quiet for a moment.

"I couldn't be that brave," Alvina finally said. "I was scared to death when Lawrence and I boarded the train. I've had him behind me every step of the way until now, and I was still scared out of my wits. Now I don't have him, and not only am I scared out of my wits, but I don't even know what to do anymore."

Beth shook her head.

"You think I wasn't scared?" Beth said incredulously. "Alvina, I was scared the whole time – I remember physically shaking as the train left the station that day, watching for my husband to emerge from the masses running and yelling at the conductor to stop the train. Hell, even now I get scared thinking that he's probably still out there, somewhere. But I do all I can do to survive, like how I'm sure you've done all you can, too. And don't you worry about what you're going to do anymore. I can tell you that much already."

"You can?" Alvina said, half-surprisedly, half-unbelievingly.

"Sure can," Beth nodded. "You're going to stay here a while until Lawrence gets back. Maybe sometimes I'll lean on you, and maybe sometimes you'll lean on me. But we'll survive all of this regardless of how scared we might be. You, me, and your baby too. Because that's all you can do, out in a place like this."

Beth stood up. Alvina looked up at her towering presence and remembered she must've been about the same height as Lawrence, if not taller.

"Here, let me grab you something to eat. I'm sure you must be starving."

And before Alvina could say anything else, Beth was out of the room.

Chapter 16

The pair did not talk much the rest of the day, as Alvina grew tired and nauseous shortly after eating. Asking if there was anywhere to lie down, Alvina found herself in Beth's bed the rest of the day, despite Alvina's insistence that she take the spare cot that Beth set up for herself in the opposite room.

"I'm not going to get a moment's rest with you and the baby on that cot, so might as well let me have it."

Alvina found it difficult to argue with this reasoning and finally decided to let it be after several minutes of arguing. Thankfully, Alvina's nausea and exhaustion alleviated after a long rest, as she spent close to sixteen hours on Beth's bed.

The following morning, Alvina woke as the sun began to rise. Once she composed herself, she got up and headed for the kitchen, hoping to make Beth a cup of tea or coffee to show her appreciation for the woman's hospitality. But when she walked into the kitchen, she found Beth was already at the kitchen table, sipping on warm tea.

"The sun's barely up," Alvina said as she sat down. "I thought I'd beat you out here for sure."

Beth shook her head as she took another sip.

"Have to wake up pretty early in the morning to beat me."

Beth poured Alvina a cup of tea.

"Déjà vu."

"I guess so."

"Say," Alvina said as she took the cup of tea into her two hands, "would you want to hear anything about me? I mean, it felt wrong to me, yesterday, to ask so much of you and give you so little in return."

"I must make some sourdough bread. If you want to tell it to me while I bake, be my guest."

Alvina felt a little slighted by the comment. She felt the gesture she was making was a large one, in which she was showing Beth both the trust she put in her as well as her own desire to further connect with this woman. Still, having put the idea out there, she thought it silly to go back on her own suggestion to speak about her past. She began to speak as Beth fished out the ingredients and tools she needed for the bread.

"I'm from Indiana. I lived in a small town there. Before I was born, my mother began seeing one of our neighbors, romantically, I mean, and to get to our house easier, the man she was seeing built a tunnel linking his house to ours. A tunnel-like bridge, that started at their house and eventually burrowed into our own."

Alvina waited for a reaction and was surprised when none came. When she said these kinds of things to others, it was all but assured they'd jump up in surprise or even call her a liar. Instead, all Beth said was,

"Interesting."

"But it wasn't easy living like that," Alvina said, sitting up a little in her chair. "Everyone in town refused to let them be. I didn't know it until years later, but apparently it was the biggest scandal in the town's history."

"And these were your parents?"

Alvina felt as though she'd been punched in the gut. Beth's guess had taken the wind out of her sails in one foul swoop.

"Yes," Alvina said as she collected herself. "Even though my mother was married to someone else at the time – an invalid who was dying in the house as the tunnel was being built – my parents had me all the same.”

“Illegitimately?”

“Illegitimately.”

“I’m sorry. That must have been tough for you,” Beth said as she poured the flour into a bowl.

“It was. Kids were awful to me at school, and the adults in the town were hardly any better. But it would’ve been a lot tougher if it weren’t for my mother. She was my best friend. She was my only friend. The teachers sided with the adults in the community, and the parents wouldn’t invite me to play with their children. I depended on my mother for everything. Even my stepfather ignored me most of the time.”

“Join the club,” Beth said jokingly. Alvina had to bite her lip to not spit back a remark. Sensing this, Beth apologized preemptively.

“Sorry Alvina,” she said, “but none of that stuff really interests me. What I really want to know is how you and your husband ended up out here on the frontier. I mean, once you’re out here, it doesn’t really matter who you are, does it?”

Alvina pinched her lips, though she understood what Beth meant.

"Well, when I was a senior in high school, I managed to make a few friends. I also worked as the church secretary, and soon after graduation they asked me if I'd want to move to Indianapolis with them."

"And you went with them?"

"Of course I went with them! God, you know how you said you'd rather have starved then gone back home? I'd rather have starved than lived in that town another day. I used that money I made as secretary and got the hell out of town. It was in Indianapolis that I learned how to take care of myself, get dressed up, put on make-up and curl my hair. And it was in Indianapolis that I met Lawrence, the very first man I ever danced with, at the very first dance I'd ever gone to."

"Hold on. You married the first man you ever danced with?"

"And you fell in love with the first man who paid you any attention, when you didn't even know what love was?"

Beth snickered at this.

"Fair enough. What happened next then?"

"I liked him enough to keep seeing him at least. But it was when I met his parents that I should've started recognizing the signs. The first time I went over, his mother waited on his father and Lawrence hand and foot. She would serve them before she even sat at the table. When the men and I ate ice cream on the patio, she and their daughter sat at a separate table inside to eat their deserts. When I asked if I could help, she wouldn't let me, saying something like it was 'her job' to make sure everyone was tended to in that house."

"Maybe it was because of that visit that I realized how much like his father Lawrence was. Although he wasn't mean about it, he expected me to do things I'd never have thought to do on my own, often for his sake. I talked about it with him a couple times, and each time he promised to try and be better, but those were the days when the war was looming in the distance and the thought of spending our last few months together squabbling was tough to swallow. So, I let him be for the most part, until he was drafted. Then, when he came home after being stationed in France, that's when he really started to act like his father. We moved in together, and he'd leave every household chore and menial task for me to do, as though he hadn't been doing them himself a month before. And he did these even when I asked him not to. Sometimes I think he was trying to get me on the hook, and when he saw I loved him, he felt comfortable asking me to be the kind of wife his mother was. A female willing to wait on him when he wanted, for as long as he wanted."

"I can't say I'm surprised, Alvina. I won't go as far as to say I know you and your husband – I don't – but what you're telling me, well I got much the same impression at the hotel, when he'd cut you off when we talked and talked about all the things 'he' wanted to do out here. I bet he started talking about homesteading as soon as you were married."

Alvina nodded.

"Homesteading is the ultimate trap for marriage. Out here, what else can you do except rely on your husband?"

"I wouldn't go that far," Alvina said. "I do think he wanted us to be happy out here."

"Was it your idea to be happy out here Alvina, or was it his?"

"It was ours," Alvina lied. Beth snorted as she stirred the flour.

"I've met a lot of women in the same position, as you and that woman who drove you over here, too. Some of them seem built to handle that lifestyle allright. Hell, a few of them even seem to really love doing it. But not you Alvina – you don't seem built for any of this."

"Well then, what can I do? I'm out here, aren't I? I can't go back to Indianapolis. I can't go back to anywhere." She was fighting to keep from tearing up now. Much of what Beth was saying Alvina had already been thinking on her own for a long time and had been desperately trying to prove untrue.

"I enjoy living here," Beth said. "Maybe I can help you learn to survive on your own, at least until Lawrence gets back for good."

"How?"

"Well for starters, you could help me make the food we eat." She gestured to the pots and pans surrounding her, which she had been rotating between as she made the bread. Alvina stood up and hurried over to the kitchen counter, trying to help as best she could. But despite Beth's instructions, she soon found herself slowing down the process more than anything, and it was with a sigh that Beth suggested Alvina instead take the laundry off the clothespins outside.

"It's like at the Sanders," Alvina thought to herself as she took the clothes off one by one. "What I lack is confidence. The biggest difference between Beth and me, for all her skills and experience, is confidence. I'd never have thought to leave her husband, like I'd never have thought to leave

Lawrence." Even thinking this gave her a bit of a jolt. "But how can I learn confidence?"

Soon she was in a full-on dialogue with herself.

"Every morning, afternoon, and evening, I should try to do something that I'd normally ask for help. Like this." Alvina thought as she plucked the last piece of clothing from the line. "Taking clothes down from the line or hanging them up there. Or even restring the clothesline if it snaps from a horse stampede. Working on the little things, and the big things, too. After all, I must learn how to do them all if I'm to live out here all alone someday."

Then she thought of her child, the life yet to be that was growing inside her. Alvina would have to learn all these things for the child, too. She'd have to act as though she knew the child all along. She'd have to know how to take care of herself well enough to do it twice as much as Beth and the Sanders and Millers had done for her.

Walking back into the cabin, Alvina nearly tripped and dropped all the clothing, catching herself at the last moment. Turning back to see what had got her, she saw one of the clotheslines had broken somehow, and now stood only half raised from the ground.

Alvina folded the laundry inside, then found Beth and told her she was going outside to restring the broken clothesline.

"Do you need help with that?" Beth asked.

"I'll figure it out as I go," Alvina said as she closed the cabin door behind her.

Chapter 17

With no instruction as to what she needed to watch over, Alvina made an effort to watch over everything in the house. In the first hour Beth was gone, Alvina went around the house surveying each piece of furniture, each tool, and each spare object that she found. Figuring she'd be staying at Beth's cabin for the foreseeable future, she did her best to familiarize herself with what went where and to figure out how she'd be able to set up a living space of her own in the cabin without displacing Beth too much. It was unthinkable that she'd take Beth's room away from another night. To prevent Beth from objecting to the idea, she moved all her belongings over to the spare cot Beth had slept in and began setting up there as best she could to make the little space a bit more homelike. She made herself tea afterwards, and though it didn't come out as well as when Beth had made it, Alvina took solace in the fact that it was drinkable.

Though Alvina sat beside the small kitchen window, her gaze remained on the cabin interior. She continued to be amazed by Beth's furnishing. Alvina doubted that she and Lawrence would ever be able to make a home quite like Beth had.

It wasn't until a loud clap of thunder came through that Alvina's gaze finally turned towards the window. What she saw as she looked out towards the prairie made her freeze.

Across the prairie, in the direction of the Sanders cabin, dark clouds had emerged. Rolling low and fast, they were on the verge of swallowing a horizon that appeared as peaceful as could be some ten minutes earlier. Another strike of lightning flickered as she watched the clouds spread, and without realizing it Alvina began to hyperventilate a little.

She gripped the windowsill.

"She'll be safe," Alvina said aloud. "She knows what she's doing."

Trying to distract herself from the sight, Alvina moved away from the window, into one of the living room chairs. There, she sat down and reached for her crochet hook, yarn and a half-finished pair of mittens she'd begun at Sanders' home. But her hands shook too much to find the next loop, and soon the yarn was too tangled in her lap to go on. Frustrated, she pushed it aside and went to grab her cup of tea. The haphazard gesture knocked the glass over, and it shattered on the floor.

"Damn it!" Alvina said. She got up to begin searching for a broom, and within moments forgot about the teacup entirely.

Though it was a far distance, and though she had never seen one before in her life, Alvina immediately recognized the strange shape in the distance. A thin, twisting funnel of grey.

"A tornado."

Momentarily, she was more awed by the sight than scared. It seemed unreal to her.

What was very real, and what startled Alvina out of the trance she'd slipped into, was the sound of a new kind of thunder that began in the distance. But it did not come in a clap like regular thunder. Instead, it came as a low thudding that shook something deep in Alvina. The thudding grew louder and louder, and soon it was close enough that Alvina could see the dining room table was beginning to shake.

Manes flying, nostrils flaring, eyes wide with terror. The herd of mustangs ran past the cabin with such fury she half expected one to come crashing into the kitchen window. Their fur took on a silver glow as lightning streaked the sky behind them, and as the last few passed by, Alvina saw that the clotheslines were draped around a mare's neck.

Alvina did not remember what happened during the next hour.

She had an impression of seeing the kitchen table begin to shake again, but not from the thudding of horse hoofs. She had the impression of a sound she'd never heard before— a low hum that steadily became a freight-train roar. She had an impression of the cabin walls beginning to shudder as the sky went dark as dusk. But what had happened to her, where she had hidden or fled to, what she'd been hit by and dodged during that hour, she could not remember. Had she dropped to the floor, clutching her head as debris battered the windows? Or had she stood there in a dumb stupor, watching it play out in awe, aware that if the tornado wanted to take her, there was nothing she could do now to stop it?

She didn't remember when the floor had stopped trembling, or when her ears had begun to ring from silence.

It was only upon opening the cabin door did Alvina snap back to life.

A rush of wet air swept in, smacking her with the scent of mud and sagebrush. The prairie was unrecognizable. The outhouse was gone entirely, a large hole in the ground being all the proof it had ever existed in the first place. The few pieces of laundry the stampede left behind were scattered about in the mud. The carcass of an animal too disfigured to be identified lay where the mud met the prairie grass. Soon Alvina was wet and cold from the wind and rain

She spent the rest of the day picking her way through the wreckage, boots sinking into the muck. She found some of the outside things seemed completely untouched by the tornado, while others were completely gone. She walked as far as she could towards Sanders' house but found no sign of Beth or her horse before turning back home.

That night, all Alvina could find the strength to do was eat half of a tin of beans and sit by the window, watching for Beth to return. She stayed beside the now-shattered window long after it got too dark to see and fell asleep in the living room chair.

The days that followed were the most silent in Alvina's life. Not only were there no other people, but the animals, too, seemed to have disappeared

with the tornado. Almost every noise came from Alvina now: from her moving things about the house back to their original positions; from her sloshing through the mud as she finished surveying the extent of the tornado's destruction. Gusts of night wind beating against the cabin walls were all that remained beyond her.

Most days she wasn't hungry and had to force herself to eat a few bites if only for the baby inside her. Most nights she could find nothing better to do than watch the door, waiting, hoping, praying Beth would come through it and put an end to her worrying. But she never did.

A week after the day of the tornado, Alvina used the last of the dry wood.

She had begun to say aloud all that she had to do. "Tomorrow, I'll have to start trying to find a way of getting to town."

"Tomorrow I'll fetch more water."

"Tomorrow, we'll look for the hens."

But every day felt like the same tomorrow, in that each tomorrow she accomplished so little of what she set out to do. There were no more hens. There was no spare dry wood hidden outside. And there was no way to get to town.

The best thing Alvina did was conserve the food supply. She found two dozen cans of food hidden in Beth's bedroom two days after the tornado and ate so little now that she'd be able to keep from starving for at least for a few months at her current rate. It wasn't that her stomach didn't hurt – it did a great deal at times – but that she simply couldn't bring herself to eat more than a few bites of food each meal. More than a few bites made her sick, and sometimes even that was too much.

About two weeks after the day of the tornado, as she was outside trying to repair a part of the roof, Alvina heard in the distance a noise that made her heart skip a beat. With great speed, she jumped down from the small stepping stool she had been standing and began surveying the horizon, trying to find where the sound of a horse galloping was coming from. In the distance, she soon spotted its source: Beth's horse, coming in the direction of Sanders' house. It was galloping in a slovenly trot and nearly tripped over itself twice as it made its way home. Even in the distance, Alvina could see how emaciated the creature had become. Its ribs pressed tight against its beaten-up fur, and a large scar of dried blood ran across its neck.

These details raised sympathy in Alvina. But as the horse approached, Alvina's grief and sorrow went out to the horse's owner alone, who was still nowhere to be seen.

Chapter 18

The first snow came early that year. It felt heavy and wet, draping the prairie in silence. The door jammed twice, and once she had to use the fire poker to chip away the ice. When she had dry wood, she boiled snow on the stove for water and rationed what little food remained.

At night, she wrapped herself in quilts, listening to the wind rattle the shutters. Sometimes she thought she heard voices outside—Beth's, or Penny's, or the laughter of children—but when she opened the door, there was only the vast, white emptiness.

Days bled into weeks. Her world became small: the stove, the bed, the horse, the window. One day, she managed to build Beth's makeshift cross to remind herself that she was real—that someone else had existed once. She brushed the snow from the wooden cross and whispered, "I'm still here, Beth. I'm still trying."

By February, the storms had quieted, but the cold had not relented. Her body ached, her belly grew heavy with life, and her hands cracked from work and frost. Still, she kept the fire alive once the wood pile dried. Still, she prayed—sometimes with words, sometimes with silence.

And when dawn broke across the prairie, painting the snow in pink and gold, Alvina stood at her window, watching the horizon. She no longer expected anyone to appear. Not Lawrence. Not the other families. Not even in spring.

But she whispered to the empty land anyway, "If the Lord still sees me, let Him send a thaw."

Outside, the prairie lay still, sleeping under its white shroud. Inside, Alvina breathed—alone, unbroken, and waiting for whatever the next day would bring.

Water had been her first issue. At the Sanders' cabin, Alvina knew one of the two wives had gone to a pump just under a quarter mile from the house every morning, often bringing one or both Millers' boys to help them carry the containers home. Though she searched as far as a mile from the house, Alvina never found such a pump on Beth's land. If it were out there at all, it was too well-hidden to find, and so she gave up on the search weeks after the tornado. From then on, she began to collect rainwater with the large wash basin in Beth's spare room. When it didn't rain, she drank tea, and when tea ran out, she began to drink whatever juices she could find in the canned food. It made her feel like an animal at times, drinking quite literally anything she could get her hands on, regardless of how gross it was, but it kept her alive all the same. It also made her appreciate rain far more than she had ever imagined she might in all her life.

It was about a month since the day of the tornado when the rain stopped. Alvina did not know how long it had been since the tornado – she'd lost count of the days by then – but she paid more than enough attention to know when it had been a full week without rain. By then the closest she got to water was eating whatever food she imagined might contain water. She stopped giving water to the horse that week, and one morning she found it had left the small pen beside the house. Alvina was almost glad about it. Better to die searching for water than in the pen. She could go with it in its search – but she was too exhausted and sick for that now. She worried if she got too far from the cabin, she might not find the strength to get back. Her decision was made and she never saw the horse again.

So it was that she began to cry when the first snow came early that year. It felt heavy and wet, draping the prairie in silence. Using the little dry wood she had managed to gather from outside, she boiled snow on the stove for water.

At night, she wrapped herself in quilts, listening to the wind rattle the shutters. Cold got into the house too easily now, through the window that had been shattered by the tornado. Though Alvina had done her best to patch the frame up, the wind and the cold got through the cover Alvina had put over the broken window. She moved her bed as far away from the window as she could get it, first to distance herself from the howling of the wind, then to get away from the seeping in of the cold.

Sometimes the wind sounded like voices — Beth's, or Penny's, or the laughter of children—but the few times Alvina was foolish enough to open the door, she was met by the same vast emptiness.

The snow made her world even smaller than it had been before. The stove, the bed, the window. That was it. She had had the sense to gather as much drywood as possible once the snowfall began, but soon there was no point in searching anymore. Everything she found began to be too wet to use. She spent the days inside, now judging how many more fires she could get out of the drywood supply she had, and how many meals she could salvage from the dwindling supply of food she still had.

One of the few warm days after the snowfall, Alvina found the small wooden cross that she had made for Beth outside the cabin. She needed to remember and to prove to herself that the woman had once existed. She wanted a conversation with Beth in hopes of gaining confidence and direction. But for some small, forlorn intent kept her from following through with the plan.

By February, the storms had quieted, but the cold had not relented. Her body began to ache more with each passing day, as her belly grew heavier and her hands more cracked from the work and the frost. She only lit fires at night now, and began to eat spices and herbs whole, for sustenance rather than taste.

Alvina no longer expected anyone to appear. Not Lawrence. Not the other families. She thought they may find her dead in the spring, a carcass hidden beneath every quilt in Beth's house. If it came to that, she wanted to write a note somewhere in the cabin, to let them know how long she had made it. After all, she hadn't rolled over and died the week after the tornado, and that had to be worth something, right? Then she'd eschew such thoughts as ridiculous, once she remembered the baby.

The baby. Food grew scarcer as it got bigger. One day, as she fantasized about the mercantile store in Medicine Bow, she realized the grave error she'd made that had likely cost her life. Her best shot had been to keep the horse alive and restore it to health as best she could, then try and ride it in to Medicine Bow for help. That had been her one chance for survival, and she had let it slip through her hands without a second thought. The horse was gone. The realization made her, for the first time in her life, consider suicide. It wasn't that she wanted to die, but to keep suffering without the hope of surviving the winter seemed absurd and cruel. Her prayers for someone to come and save her had gone unanswered long enough that her faith began to waiver. One day, without realizing it, she stopped praying altogether.

A pale sun pushed through the frost-rimmed window. She moved slowly, her joints stiff from the cold. Aloud, she whispered, "All right, Alvina, one more day. Let's make it count." It was what she said to herself every morning now.

She heated the last of the snowmelt on the stove. When she went to make breakfast, she found she had run out of canned food the night before. She rummaged for more food perfunctorily, but she knew she'd find none. Alvina had been living in Beth's cabin for nearly five months now, and in that time, she had learned every nook and cranny of the house by heart. She knew all the spots Beth had hidden food in, and many more Beth herself had likely not even been aware of. After checking the last spot in the house and finding it empty, Alvina clapped her hands. That was it then. More than anything, she felt relieved.

She looked through the non-shattered window. It was a fair-weather day.

"A parting gift." Alvina said aloud. "If I had the horse, I might have made it all the way to Medicine Bow on a day like this."

She pulled on a coat that no longer buttoned, wrapping a thick wool blanket around her belly and legs. She slipped the cold fingers of her left hand into her dress pocket, then opened the door with her right hand.

The world had begun to thaw.

The wind was gentle against her face, and the sun warmed her ever so slightly. In a couple weeks, the snow might have melted enough for her to scavenge some cattails for food. She knew of a small pond about a mile from the cabin, but she had not thought of going there to gather food until it was far too late.

Not that it mattered now. She figured she'd be dead in a week. The idea of somehow growing even hungrier and more nauseous than she had now came to mind. She did her best to repress it.

"No more scraping snow or praying for rain at least."

No more huddling by an unlit fireplace for warmth. No more sickness throughout the day. No more worrying that she had let the baby down.

The prairie wind hummed softly outside as Alvina walked further from the cabin. At first, she had only meant to step outside while she had the strength to still do so. She wanted to see the world one last time and appreciate whatever there was to see out here, before she was too starved and nauseous to think straight. But she kept walking. Despite the pain in her legs, and despite the kicks in her stomach urging her to return baby and host to the warmer inside, Alvina kept walking. After some time walking, she realized she had no intention of going back. This was to be it...

"I'm sorry you didn't get to be born," she said, putting one hand on the top of her outstretched belly as she walked. "I'm sorry you don't get the chance to go to school and make friends and laugh and eat a good hot meal on a cold winter day. Or to know what it feels like to have the sunlight warm you, or to be told 'I love you' by someone important to you. I'm sorry I couldn't give that to you."

The baby had stopped kicking by then. Alvina wondered without emotion if it had died. Then it gave her a hard thump, and she couldn't help laughing as she heeled over in pain.

"I don't blame you. There's a lot to see out here. I would be angry if I didn't get to see it either."

She leaned against a small tree and began to describe the sensation of her hands against the bark to the baby, as though to give it a last chance to know what living was like. When she found no more to say about the tree, she talked of the sunlight that flecked through its leaves. Then the mountains in the distance, and the prairie before them. And the sun and the clouds. And a rabbit in the distance, scurrying across it all, the first sign of a life beyond her own Alvina had seen in five months.

As she tracked it with her eyes, her vision began to go. Black splotches leaked into the view, then pain began to radiate throughout her body. She leant harder against the tree, until she was hardly standing at all. This was it – she was certain this was dying – and she was grateful it wasn't as painful as she'd imagined. She closed her eyes and let a breath out, as at peace with herself as she'd ever been in her life.

Then she had a contraction.

Chapter 19

Though she had hardly gone farther than a mile from the cabin, it took Alvina the better part of an hour before she made it back inside. In that time, she alternated between sprinting, jogging, and walking back towards the cabin whenever the pain was bearable enough to move. Malnourished and freezing, she found herself wanting to give up nearly every time the pain became too much to keep moving. If only she let herself sit down – but then she knew if she sat, she'd never give up. Finally, after a dash of a little under a hundred yards, Alvina made it into the house and shut the cabin door behind her. Though there was no fire going, Beth's cabin was still far warmer than the outside, and Alvina might have well felt relief and even pride then had a new pain not emerged that caused her to topple over and scream without reserve. It was like no pain she'd ever had before – nothing could compare to it, and she wished very much, then, that she had died leaning against the tree.

Once the pain reduced enough that Alvina could open her eyes again and pull herself up from the floor and into one of the chairs, she noticed an odd smell in the air and a more concentrated level of sweat along one of her thighs. Only, when she looked at the thigh, she realized it was not sweat that she was looking at.

"So, I'm one of them now," she thought to herself, realizing her water had broken back at the tree.

No midwife. No husband. No one within a five-mile radius. For the first time in a long time, she thought of Penny and Lillian, and how they would've known what was happening to her now, and what was to come next. Now, she had only the baby to let her know.

Another contraction tore through Alvina's body. She gripped the edge of the table and clenched her teeth. It shook her to life, reminding her not only of what was going on, but what was yet to come.

"The midwife ties the umbilical cord with twine in two places," a friend at the freight office had once told her, years ago, during an idle conversation about motherhood. "Then they cut between them with clean scissors." What was that woman's name? She could see the woman's face now – she and Alvina had been friends for a year or so – but she couldn't remember the woman's name for the life of her now. Another contraction made her scream involuntarily.

Alvina's breath soon became shallow bursts. She righted herself from the prone position she had been in and pulled herself up to her feet with a strength she hardly believed herself to have. She saw now that this could well be the last time she stood on her feet again, and so made haste to find the ball of coarse twine and the pair of sewing scissors she knew lay in the lone sewing basket.

The contractions were closer now, sharp and insistent, rolling through her in waves. She sat back down and put the scissors and twine on the table beside her. Her body rebelled at this, the pain doubling within moments of being off her feet, begging her to stand up again and alleviate her from the suffering. But she had no strength to stand now. So, she did the next best thing she could think of and began to cry.

The pain kept getting to the point where Alvina thought it could not possibly get worse, only for it to get worse again. Her breathing was now exclusively hyperventilating, and without realizing it she had begun shaking all over. The few moments she caught her breath, she shrieked. Her shrieks were so raw that Alvina could hardly believe it was herself making the noises, and not some dying beast in the distance. Once, a sharp wave of pain moved her to try and get back on her feet to alleviate the pain. But she had guessed right before – her legs were completely shot – and Alvina fell over herself to the floor the moment she put weight on her one foot. The pain multiplied instantaneously. She shrieked even louder.

Tossing and turning, wailing and moaning, Alvina did not think of anything but the pain. She did not know how long she lay there, praying for it all to be over one way or another. It might have been hours, but it felt like days, and she might have gone on writhing pain had a strange noise cut her off as she inhaled to scream again.

"Oh God," she gasped, half sobbing, half laughing. "Oh God. Oh God. Oh God. Oh God."

It became like a mantra to Alvina, and soon she found herself at last pushing to get the baby out. She pushed and cried for twenty minutes as the crying slowly grew louder. Then the room went quiet except for Alvina's breathing and moans.

She pushed harder. The room stayed quiet. She pushed harder and harder, until she thought her organs would fall out alongside the baby once it came out, but then she didn't care if they did. As more time passed between the last muffled cry,

Alvina began to pray to God that the baby would live. Let the baby live. Kill her and let it live. Let it take her intestines out with it, only don't let it die along with her. Let her hold the baby for one minute, screaming and wriggling about her arms as though there were anywhere to go beyond the claustrophobic walls of this goddamned cabin, and then God could take her and do what he wanted with her. Send her to heaven or hell – if she could hold the baby alive for one moment, she'd take it all without complaint. Just don't let it be dead.

With an intuition she neither understood nor questioned, Alvina knew when the last push had come and gone, and she scooped from beneath her the still mum body. It was warm and wet. As Alvina brought the body towards her, she felt certain it was dead. It was as still as a doll, and when Alvina saw its face, with its peacefully shut eyes and mouth, she squeezed the body tight to her and began to scream again from a pain even newer to her than birth.

After the faintest of wriggles, the baby opened its mouth and began to cry alongside its mother. Her vision blurred by tears, and the baby's cries drowned out by Alvina's own screams, the mother thought her baby dead a full minute before she at last saw the little mouth joining in her wailing. A tear fell from her face onto the baby, and it wriggled and cried harder in its discomfort. More tears fell.

The baby was thinner than any Alvina had ever seen in her life, and a pang of guilt overcame her as she realized it was her own failure to thrive on the prairie that had caused this. But it was alive, and fearing it may not be alive much longer, or that she herself may die, soon, from God knew what at this point, Alvina gathered the baby and brought it against her chest.

The baby, slick and red, did not like the movement, and began to show a new zest for life as it squirmed wildly to be free of Alvina's grasp. As meek and as gaunt as it was, Alvina felt she had never seen a sorrier, more pathetic creature in her life. She took the scissor beside her, cut one of the quilts, and swaddled the baby.

Then she noticed the cord—thick, pale, still attached. She laughed without knowing why.

Her fingers fumbled as she reached for the twine and shook as she tied the first piece of twine tightly near the baby's belly, then another farther up toward herself.

As she lifted the scissors, a sudden cramp seized her abdomen. But instead of another baby, a heavy, wet mass slid out of her body. Relief washed over her, and riding this feeling she seized the strings tighter and carefully cut between the two tied sections of twine. To her surprise, there was no pain.

The baby's cries began to soften to whimper. Alvina sat there for a long moment, breathing deeply, trying to steady herself. Her arms shook as she lifted the baby higher, cradling the tiny head against her shoulder. "You must be hungry," she said softly. But there was nothing there for either of them to eat.

Then she remembered another thing her friend had told her about the single skill every newborn had no matter how young they were. She loosened her gown, guiding the baby toward her breast. The first attempts were awkward—she laughed weakly through her exhaustion. When the baby finally latched, she exhaled in relief.

Her hair clung to her damp forehead as she watched the baby feed, and her arms ached from holding the child, yet she could not bear to set the baby down. A boy so tiny she could hardly believe it was alive – but then, was it a boy? Alvina realized she hadn't checked yet, and unwrapped part of the patchwork swaddle. No, it was a girl. Alvina smiled weakly, laughed a little, then began to cry quietly. Alvina realized she, too, was hungry, and that there was nothing for her to eat, and no one for her to turn to. She pushed the thought from her mind as best she could, turning towards the window to see what time of day it was.

The prairie was dark now, only the moon casting pale light through the small window. She could hear the wind whistling through the broken window and feel the room around them slowly growing colder. Alvina desperately wished for a fire, and assured the baby she would go out looking for firewood tomorrow.

"Naoma," she said suddenly. "That was the name of the woman," the woman who had told Alvina about cutting umbilical cords and newborn instincts in casual conversation over half a decade ago. Alvina remembered that the name was from the Book of Ruth. She looked down at the baby.

"How do you like the sound of that? Naoma. Naoma Bertha," she added spontaneously.

The baby stirred at the sound, letting out a tiny sigh. Alvina took it as a sign of agreement. She smiled. "Naoma Bertha Hursting."

She tried to stand up and found she still could not. So, they were to die together in this very position. For some reason, the thought didn't unnerve Alvina as much as she had thought it would. In the last hour, a tranquility had overcome her like none she had ever known. Neither the cold of the coming night, nor the fading sun in her eyes bothered her now. She felt she was past it all now. Life. She had done everything she could, and now the sights and sounds around her she looked at with the amusement of someone living on borrowed time.

She turned away from the window, back towards the baby. She watched as the baby's small chest rose and fell against her own, a steady rhythm that furthered her own sense of peace. Alvina savored the sound of the baby's breathing, as hushed as it was. It was the first time in many months she didn't feel alone.

Chapter 20

It was a rare, almost eerie pause in the winter storms. Though the wind still blew hard, and though it was still slightly below freezing, a single small prairie schooner could be seen traversing the snowy plains that lined the western edge of Mule Creek County. Inside the schooner were a man and a woman, bundled from head to toe. Their eyes watered from the wind in their faces while their breath plumed in front of them.

Despite the fact every beaten path was well-hidden beneath the melting layers of snow, the schooner navigated the prairies with a knowing precision. The riders were familiar with the route, as it was the fifth consecutive winter they had gone about checking every cabin scattered across Mule Creek country.

It was late into the day when, a few minutes after leaving the Sanders' cabin, riding along the prairie, the woman pointed out a house in the distance she knew they hadn't yet checked on.

"Aren't we going to Beth's cabin?"

"Why should we?" said the man. "We know she lived alone."

"Yes, but what if someone is squatting there?"

The man said the possibility was beyond slim. There was a confrontational quality to his voice as he said it, the woman noted. She couldn't blame him. He had been one of the men called in to identify Beth's body when the news of her death broke.

"I don't want to go and see her house suspended as it was when she left," the man added. "It would be like walking into a ghost's house."

"But what if someone is there? We'd never let ourselves live it down, if someone was there and we ignored them."

"There's no one there. Besides, we know there are other houses with people in them that still need to be checked. Going to her cabin would be a waste of time, and we only have so much time before another storm comes."

He gestured towards the horizon, where a pack of clouds hovered ominously in the distance. The clouds had been approaching the schooner all day, if only at a crawling pace. The man hadn't thought to worry too much about them, though. After the Sanders cabin, the rest of the houses they were to check on were much closer to town, so that it would be no more than a mile they'd have to go before lights and shoveled paths would lead them home. Beth's cabin, however, would take them straight towards the clouds.

"Can't we just check?"

"I don't want to get caught out here when it's dark."

"We'd be long gone by then. It won't take that long."

The man looked at the western horizon, gauging how much sunlight they had left. An hour and a half worth, he guessed.

"Evans, please."

At last, the man let out a large sigh, then turned the reigns of the two mules towards the cabin the woman had pointed out. The preacher had a very difficult time saying 'no' to his wife.

-

Yet the closer the schooner drew to the house, the more Preacher Evans felt his judgment had been right and that they were wasting their time. Even from a hundred yards away, anyone who had been on the frontier long enough could make out the signs of a cabin long abandoned. A corner of the roof collapsing in on itself. No light radiating from the cabin's windows. No smoke rising from its single chimney. Not a single path of snow shoveled out.

The mules were trembling from the long day's effort as well as the cold by the time the schooner reached the cabin. The preacher knew this would have to be their last stop of the day.

"I told you," Preacher Evans said as they approached, unable to contain himself. "No one's here."

He made to turn the mules around again, but his wife, Betsy, grabbed one of his wrists before he could do so. He pulled on the reigns in surprise, so that the mules came to a stop in moments. The schooner thus came to a stop some twenty paces from Beth's cabin. Before the preacher could berate his wife for her recklessness, Betsy jumped out of the cart and began to walk towards the cabin.

"Betsy!" he yelled out after her as she walked on. "It's going to be dark soon. We don't have time for this."

But he knew she wasn't coming back now. Once his wife put her mind to something, there was little anyone could do to stop her. So, with another groan of exasperation, the preacher brought the mules back toward the cabin again. He brought them to a stop beside the small stable Beth's horse must have lived out of, where he tethered each to one of the stakes. His wife was peering into the lone window of the cabin's front wall by the time the preacher approached her. Tensing up a little at the sight, he noticed the faintest of snowfall had already begun.

"Betsy, this is ridiculous."

"I can see a pile of trash in there, heaped up in the corner." She had her face pressed up the single small glass window within the cabin's front wall. "Beth wasn't the type of woman to let her house get like that."

The preacher shook his head.

"There's no way you can see something like that in there. It's too dark – your eyes are probably playing tricks on you."

But when the preacher grabbed his wife's hand, she shook him off with a resilience that almost scared him.

"I'm going in," she said firmly.

The preacher reached toward the door handle, then shook it hard to show it wouldn't budge.

"Locked. The latch must be frozen shut."

Betsy looked at the handle quizzically for a moment, gauging her options.

"Let's try the back," she said, turning to go round the cabin. Knowing the futility of resistance by now, the preacher resignedly followed his wife. As he did so, he looked toward the western horizon again. The sun had lowered a good deal since leaving the Sanders' cabin. They'd have to be quick.

In one of the two openings in the cabin's rear wall, a large quilt was pinned up against the window frame. Betsy touted this as more proof that someone must have been there since Beth's death.

"Maybe a looter," the preacher said skeptically. Still, it was enough reason to at least go inside and expel any doubts. Besides, the preacher knew he'd have to go in the cabin now. If there were squatters inside, he didn't want Betsy facing them alone.

He pulled a hunting knife from one of his pockets, then cut through the quilt. They made their way into the house, the preacher entering first, then helping his wife step through the opening and into the house.

The inside was only marginally warmer than the outdoors. With no lights besides the little sunlight that crept in from the windows, it took time for their eyes to adjust to the dimness. When shapes became more than silhouettes, they saw frost clinging to almost every household item scattered about. Tins of food licked clean were stacked in a pile furthest from the window.

"Hello?" the preacher called out. No one in the cabin responded. He creeped out of the back room, through the doorway, and into the main room of the cabin. His wife followed a few feet behind him.

Betsy had been right. There were ample signs someone had survived inside the cabin as recently as a week ago. The fire pit was black from soot alone, with very little frost crusting its edges.

Dishes inside a water-filled basin were only partially covered with mold. No animal droppings or carcasses were immediately visible.

"What's that smell?" Betsy said, the strong sickly-sweet smell of ammonia making her eyes water. Walking about, she saw a dark brown shape that lay on the floor which, the closer she got, the stronger the smell became. It didn't look like something man-made, but then it didn't look like a carcass or droppings either.

The preacher picked up the single framed photo in the house. It was a much younger and more joyous face, but he recognized it as Beth's. Despite his best efforts, the images came back to his mind he'd worked for weeks to forget.

When they found Beth's body, the crook in her neck was that of someone who had been dropped from at least three stories up. He had been told how her belongings had been found scattered about haphazardly while her body was still virtually intact, so they knew it couldn't have been robbers or animals. But what a woman like that had been doing outside in that kind of weather was beyond the preacher's comprehension. Though they weren't particularly close with her, the preacher and his wife had known Beth for the five years she had lived on the frontier. She was a resourceful, savvy woman. She would've known how reckless it was to be outside during a tornado.

A sound. A sound so faint that it might have been a settling board or the wind slipping under the eaves. But as faint as it was, both heard it, and both jumped in astonishment and fear. The preacher dropped the picture. Betsy let out the beginning of a squeal before catching herself. They looked at each other, then waited.

Frozen as they were, the sound did not repeat itself for another minute.

"That's a baby," Betsy said at last, recognizing the sound. Each peered around the room. Yet, even though they could search the entirety of the cabin within thirty seconds, no one found any sign of life in the house after nearly ten minutes of looking. They might have spent much longer looking, too, and had a third cry not come. It was the preacher who found the pair. Half-slumped against the bedpost in the room opposite, the preacher and his wife had unknowingly looked over Alvina half a dozen times. Several quilts were wrapped around every part of her body, so that from afar she looked like little more than a stack of them thrown beside the bed. Her breathing was so faint, too, that the stack hardly moved up and down with each breath she took.

"Betsy, come quick!"

Alvina was in the preacher's arms by the time Betsy came in.

"Dear Lord… it's Alvina Hursting."

But Alvina looked nothing like the woman they had met several months earlier. Her skin was chalk-white except for two high, dangerous blotches of fever on her cheeks. Her lips were cracked, almost blue. Her eyes were sunken, hollowed into dark caverns of exhaustion

When she finally tried to speak, her voice cracked into nothing but a hoarse breath.

"Lawrence?"

She tried to say more but was overcome by a violent fit of coughing. Then the crying from before came back, louder. Noticing a bulge in one of the quilts wrapped beneath Alvina's chin, the preacher peeled the covering away, revealing the top half of a gaunt newborn. Its face was red and puckered.

Instinctually, Betsy came to the preacher and picked up the newborn, trying to soothe in it in her arms as she had soothed her own children decades ago. The baby, naked once the quilt was stripped away, squirmed weakly in Betsy's grip for no more than a few moments, quickly tiring itself out.

"Evans, it's half dead. Cold to the touch, and I can see each of its little ribs."

"She's burning up," the preacher said, putting the back of his hand to Alvina's forehead. "Fever. Dehydration. Probably mild hypothermia, too."

"If we hadn't come –"

"But we did," the preacher interrupted his wife. "And now we need to get them out of here. We need to help them warm up and get some food and water quick."

To his wife's confusion, the preacher began to strip layer after layer away from his body. It was only when he began trying to get Alvina into one of his coats did she understand.

"She might have clothes of her own –"

"We don't have time to look."

Nodding, Betsy knelt to help. Preacher Evans motioned her away.

"Wrap the baby. As many quilts as you can."

She stepped back, then began to bundle the baby as best she could with each of the quilts. It fussed throughout.

"I'm done. Let me help you," Betsy said once the baby was swaddled with five different quilts. Again, the preacher motioned his wife to say back.

"Go bring the mules around to the window we came through. With all these clothes on her, I won't be able to carry her much farther than that."

Betsy looked at her husband momentarily, hesitating, then ran from the room.

There had been another reason the preacher did not want his wife helping him. Putting his last coat on to Alvina, the preacher warily noted that her breathing was uneven and shallow. Even through the clothing, he could feel how gaunt Alvina was, too. And he had understated how bad her fever was. He worried that, even if they got her to shelter, the woman wouldn't survive longer than a week. But for now, all he could do was get her out of here.

To his surprise, Alvina opened her mouth to speak.

"Lawrence, you have to –"

But again a fit of coughs interrupted her, and the preacher shushed her as gently as he could.

"Don't talk, Alvina. You don't have the energy to."

"Evans, I'm here!" Betsy shouted from outside the smashed open window.

Evans wrapped the last spare quilt around Alvina, then went to lift her. Her head lolled against his arm as he did, and the numerous layers of clothes made it awkward to hold her. Thankfully she was thin enough that he could carry her to and through the window without having to stop.

The wind nearly knocked the preacher over as he emerged from the cabin. To his astonishment, the path to the schooner was hardly visible through the flurries and the suppressed sunlight. He nearly fell over himself after his first step out the window, too, the layer of snow surrounding the cabin having risen significantly while they were inside. The long stretch of darkening clouds was now overtop of them, covering the sky in all directions. He searched for the sun and saw it hardly peeking over the horizon. They had stayed too long.

A pang of pride overcame Betsy as she watched her husband carry the shrunken woman to the schooner. She was wrapped from head to toe as best as the preacher could manage, while he had on nothing more than his base layer. He lay Alvina in the back of the schooner as gently as he could, then hopped beside his wife. She gave him one of her own coats, which he slipped on as quickly as he could. He noticed how tightly she was still holding the baby.

"It's a miracle this baby's alive," Betsy murmured. Tears slipped down her cold-stung cheeks and fell onto the baby's face, which squinted and cried again.

"It's a miracle either of them is alive," the preacher said as he whipped on the backs of the mules. But as they began to trudge through the snow, he could only think of how it wouldn't be a miracle if the mother and child were simply to die a few days from now, as the preacher secretly suspected both would. It wouldn't be a miracle, either, if all four of them were to die out here in this snowstorm. Within minutes of leaving the cabin, the sky had grown so dark that the preacher could hardly see the mules in front of them. He turned to look back toward the cabin, questioning whether they ought to have stayed the night at the deserted cabin, if only to save themselves. But

Beth's cabin was nowhere to be seen by then, and he knew that turning around to go back would be to try and find a needle in a haystack. Without lights on inside, they'd nearly have to run into the cabin to find it. Yet the town was still half a dozen miles away.

"We need to stop at the Widmeyers'," his wife said, clutching the baby even tighter to her breast. She had evidently had the same train of thought.

"We'll make it," he said in as reassuring a voice as he could manage, though he knew even the Widmeyers' cabin was still a couple miles away. He whipped harder on the mules as they began to slow in the growing layers of snow. Despite his best efforts, he was now violently shaking from the cold.

The baby began to cry that same cry that had helped the preacher and his wife locate the mother and baby an hour ago. Only now, despite Betsy's best efforts, it could not be placated. In the whirling, raging snowstorm, its cries grew louder and louder, and the preacher beat on the reigns harder and harder. Soon he could no longer see the backs of the mules. His wife began to sing to the child.

The schooner came within feet of hitting a large, wayward pine tree. Instinctively turning the reins away from the obstacle, with his eyes watering and his hands numb, the preacher realized he hadn't the slightest idea where they were, or where they were going.

P.S.

This is not where Alvina's story ends.

What comes next is how her strength is tested in new ways, her choices shaped by everything she survived.

Her journey continues in Part Two, coming in 2026.

About the author

Kay Perrin, PhD: A Life of Dedication, Adventure, and Lifelong Learning

Born and raised in Denver, Colorado, Kay Perrin's life has been marked by her academic achievements, professional success, and global adventures. After graduating with her nursing degree, Kay went on to work as a full-time nurse. However, after over a decade in this field, she repivoted her life in a new direction, enrolling at the University of South Florida (USF) in her 40's. There she earned her Master's and PhD in Public Health, then continued on at USF as a faculty member for 26 years, where she rose to the position of Associate Dean of Public Health.

While employed at USF, Kay worked to further public health education at a local and international level. Her work abroad most notably included a six-month trip to Pune, India, where she taught nursing and supervised student rotations as a Fulbright Scholar. By the time of her retirement, Kay had authored five public health textbooks and helped create Florida's first undergraduate Public Health degree at USF.

Following her retirement, Kay has begun channeling her energy and creativity into new outlets. She adores spending time with her two sons, Scott and Andrew, as well as her five grandchildren and one dog. In her free time, Kay walks several miles each day, takes comedy classes, and writes historical fiction novels.

Her debut novel, The Spinster That I Once Knew, is based on her great-aunt's diary. Her second novel, Alvina: Strong and Determined, focuses on her maternal grandmother's journey of homesteading in Wyoming. In 2026, her third novel, Naoma: Stamina With Grace, explores her mother's life.

Discussion Questions

1. What is a situation in today's world that parallels the behavior of Alvina's parents that made them outcast family in their small Midwest town?
2. Have you ever had the opportunity to go against the rules to help someone? Think back to how the teacher abused Alvina in her time of need.
3. Do you think that Alvina made the right decision to marry Lawrence? Do you have female relatives that married men after knowing them for a short time?
4. If you were alive in the 1920s, would you have volunteered to live on a homestead in Wyoming for five years to claim 560 acres at no cost? Why or why not?
5. When you think about Alvina's life on the homestead, what part would have been the hardest for you in the same situation?
6. How would you have advised Alvina, your friend, when it came time to move from the homestead? What were her options?

7. Have you experienced a time in your life when you were afraid to stand up to a person to make your point with strength and determination? How were you changed by that situation?

8. The author inherited 560 acres in Wyoming from her grandparents. The property looks much like it did in the1920s – no house, no trees. In 2024, the author paid to have a well drilled and pump installed. What would you do with this property?